*THE TRI*

D0251822

NANCY DREW MYSTERY STORIES®

# *THE TRIPLE HOAX*

## *by*
## *Carolyn Keene*

### Illustrated by
### Ruth Sanderson

## WANDERER BOOKS
*New York*

Copyright © 1979 by Stratemeyer Syndicate
All rights reserved
including the right of reproduction
in whole or in part in any form
Published by Wanderer Books
A Simon & Schuster Division of
Gulf & Western Corporation
Simon & Schuster Building
1230 Avenue of the Americas
New York, New York 10020

Manufactured in the United States of America
10 9 8 7 6 5 4 3 2

Library of Congress Cataloging in Publication Data

Keene, Carolyn, pseud.
The triple hoax.

(Nancy Drew mystery stories ; 57)
SUMMARY: Nancy Drew and friends Bess and George
track a group of swindlers and kidnappers from New York
to Mexico City to Los Angeles where they finally
solve the mystery of the Triple Hoax.
[1. Mystery and detective stories]   I. Title.
PZ7.K23Nan no. 57          [Fic]          79-17214

ISBN 0-671-95490-3
ISBN 0-671-95512-8 pbk.

Also available in Wanderer Hardcover Edition

# *Contents*

*Hoax:* An act intended to trick or dupe; something accepted or established by fraud or fabrication.

*Webster's New Collegiate Dictionary*

# 1

## A Sudden Trip

"Dad! Aunt Eloise wants me to come to New York immediately to solve a mystery!" eighteen-year-old Nancy Drew called out excitedly.

Carson Drew, a well-known attorney in River Heights, looked fondly at his attractive, titian-haired daughter as she returned to the breakfast table. "What kind of mystery?"

Nancy waved a special delivery letter that the mailman had brought. "Listen to this. I'll read it to you.

"Dear Nancy,
A close friend of mine, Mrs. Annabella Richards, has been swindled. She taught in the same school I do, but left a few years ago

to marry a wealthy man. He died not long ago, and Annabella is a rich widow. I won't give you any more details now, but I certainly hope you can visit me and help her. Bring your friends Bess and George if you like, and say hello to my brother for me.

Lots of love,
Aunt Eloise"

"Well, Dad, what do you think?" Nancy asked.

Mr. Drew laughed. "I think that you want to go and I see no reason why you shouldn't. The mystery sounds interesting. I'll be eager to hear more about it."

Nancy jumped up, kissed her father, and hurried to the telephone. First she called George Fayne, a slender, dark-haired girl who enjoyed her boyish name. Then she contacted George's cousin Bess Marvin, who was a slightly plump, pretty blond with dimples. Both girls loved to help Nancy on her mystery cases, and together they had solved many of them.

Bess and George were keen to join Nancy on her trip to New York. Their parents, after some persuasion, furnished the money. It was arranged that the young sleuths would leave River Heights the following day.

As Nancy packed her bag, the Drews' lovable housekeeper, Mrs. Hannah Gruen, came into the girl's bedroom. She had lived with Nancy and her father since Mrs. Drew's death, when Nancy was three years old, and had been like a mother to her. The two had shared many secrets and adventures.

"Nancy," Hannah said, "judging from past performances, you're likely to get into all sorts of ticklish situations. I beg you to be careful. You know you're an indispensable member of this household!"

Nancy chuckled. "I'm glad to find out I'm really needed here. But you know, when I'm working on a case, it's pretty hard to keep from running into danger."

"I know," Hannah agreed. "Your father and I will be wishing you the best of luck all the way."

The following afternoon Mr. Drew drove the girls to the airport. They boarded a plane that took them directly to La Guardia Airport in New York. After debarking, they were met in the terminal by Nancy's tall, attractive Aunt Eloise and her friend.

"Nancy, it's wonderful to see you!" Miss Drew exclaimed. "And Bess and George. I want all of you to meet Mrs. Annabella Richards."

After hugs, kisses, and excited welcomes, the group walked outside and awaited Mrs. Richards's chauffeur-driven car. Ten minutes passed, but it did not arrive.

The annoyed woman frowned. "Roscoe is always so prompt and reliable," she said. "I can't understand why he isn't here."

"Could you tell us something about your mystery while we're waiting?" Nancy asked.

Mrs. Richards nodded. But before she could begin, a strange man walked up to her. "Are you Mrs. Richards?" he asked.

"Yes."

"Your chauffeur, Roscoe, sent me to tell you your car won't start."

"Won't start!" the woman exclaimed. "He drove me here a little while ago and there was nothing wrong with the car. In fact, it was serviced recently."

"I don't know anything about that, ma'am," the stranger said. "Roscoe suggests you go home by taxi." With that, the man turned and walked off.

Mrs. Richards frowned. "I don't understand it," she remarked. "Well, I guess we'd better go."

She summoned a limousine and the five climbed inside. As the car pulled away, Mrs. Richards said, "I suppose Eloise has told you a little of my situation."

Nancy had a sudden hunch. It might be best if Mrs. Richards did not reveal her story for the taxi driver to hear.

She leaned over and whispered into the woman's ear, "Don't reveal any of your secrets now." Mrs. Richards nodded and changed the subject. The conversation became general until the

5

group arrived at Aunt Eloise's attractive apartment.

Then Mrs. Richards went on with her story. "My husband was very kindhearted and charitable. He donated money to large and small organizations, and even to individuals. After his death I carried on this tradition, but the work became too much for me. I finally hired my husband's former secretary, who promised to take care of everything so I could go on vacation. About that time, a travel agent contacted me and offered a wonderful bargain world tour."

"Sounds fabulous," Bess said dreamily.

"It did," Mrs. Richards agreed. "The agent showed me enticing literature and I fell for it. A few days later he brought the plane tickets and hotel accommodations, and I paid him $3,000. It was too bad that I had not investigated the whole thing."

"Why, was something wrong?" George asked.

"Indeed it was. When I went to the airport, the airline named on the ticket had a counter, but no such flight."

"How dreadful!" Bess exclaimed. "And you paid all this money to a swindler?"

"Yes, I did," Mrs. Richards said sadly. She turned to Nancy. "Please help me find that man! I contacted the police, but nothing came of it. Maybe your friends Bess and George can help you. Your Aunt Eloise tells me you're wonderful young sleuths."

The girls smiled and accepted the challenge at once.

"What was the travel agent's name and where was he located?" Nancy asked.

"He gave his name as Henry Clark and his address as 14 Canalee Road in Queens. The police checked it and found both to be phony."

"What did he look like?"

"Oh, he was tall, handsome, and had a dark beard. He was a smooth talker and very pleasant."

"Did you pay him by check or in cash?"

"Cash. He said the airline would not take a personal check."

George spoke up. "He probably skipped town with your money."

"That's what the police think. They doubt they'll ever find him. Perhaps you girls can unravel this mystery for me."

"We'll do our best," Nancy promised. "Unfortunately we have very little to go on."

"I understand that," Mrs. Richards said. "And now I'd better get home." She turned to Miss Drew. "Eloise, may I call my apartment and see if Roscoe had the car fixed?"

"Of course."

Mrs. Richards dialed the number and spoke to her housekeeper, Trudie. Suddenly the girls saw her turn ashen white.

"That's terrible!" Mrs. Richards cried out. "I'll be right over. I hope nothing has happened to Roscoe!"

She put down the receiver. "Trudie told me a man called the apartment. He said I would never see my car again. Before she could ask about Roscoe, the stranger hung up. Oh, dear! I hope my chauffeur hasn't met with foul play!"

"So do I," Aunt Eloise said sympathetically. "I'll get a taxi for you. Let us know what happened, and if we can be of any help."

After the distressed woman had left, Aunt Eloise said she would start dinner. The girls followed her to the kitchen and helped prepare the meal.

While they were eating, Miss Drew announced, "With all this excitement, I almost forgot that I have four tickets to a magic show tonight. It's given by a group called the Hoaxters."

"That sounds interesting," Bess remarked.

Aunt Eloise nodded. "Annabella saw it and said it was fascinating. Incidentally, there is a big surprise in the show. She wouldn't tell me what it is."

The girls were eager to see the performance, which proved, indeed, to be most unusual. A dark-haired sleight of hand man with a perky mustache, listed on the program as Ronaldo Jensen, started with an amazing card trick. He asked people in the audience to name a card, then time after time he pulled the correct one out of his pack.

8

"How in the world does he do that?" Bess whispered to Nancy.

"I wish I knew," the girl replied.

Next, a young woman was brought onto the stage in a gilt chair with red plush upholstery. Her eyes were blindfolded. Another performer held a black cloth in front of her legs for a moment. When he pulled it away, her legs were gone!

The audience gasped, while the girl held her arms up high. The magician put the black cloth in front of them. Seconds later, the arms had disappeared!

"Oh, this is dreadful!" Bess cried out. "That poor girl!"

George grinned. "Don't be silly. You know it's only a trick!"

Her cousin settled back. "But it seems so real!"

Now the man held the cloth in front of the girl's body. When he removed it, the chair was empty!

"Oh!" Bess exclaimed.

Even Nancy was perplexed. She had seen many magic shows and knew how several of the tricks were done. But she could not figure out how this disappearing act was possible.

As the performer gradually restored the girl, section by section, Bess heaved a great, audible sigh of relief.

"Feel better now?" George teased her.

"Much."

Next, another member of the troupe stepped from the wings to the edge of the stage. He announced, "We are now inviting a few people from the audience to come forward and see how we do our tricks!"

At once Bess jumped out of her seat and started up the aisle, handbag swinging over her arm. She was one of the first to reach the stage.

The sleight of hand man accepted ten people, including Bess, then repeated his card trick. It was just as puzzling to the onlookers as it had been before, even though they were now standing very close to him.

Suddenly the magician pulled a watch out of a young man's ear. He compared it with his own watch. "Seems to be an hour ahead. Get it? A-head," he quipped, grinning.

As everyone laughed, the magician put the watch into his own pocket, telling the visitor he would return it later.

"See this!" he said, and produced a wallet from inside another man's collar.

"Hey, that was in my hip pocket which was buttoned!" the amazed fellow shouted. "How'd you do that?"

The magician chuckled. "We invited you to watch. You tell me! And don't worry about your wallet. It will be returned to you right after the show."

Bess was fascinated. Suddenly it occurred to her: Would these people really receive their property back?

She felt for her own handbag. It was gone! She stared intently at the sleight of hand man. He did not have the bag, and it was nowhere in sight!

# 2

## *Bess's Strange Caller*

Bess startled everyone on stage by crying out, "Someone has taken my handbag!"

A woman standing near her exclaimed, "And my expense account notebook is gone!"

George jumped up and announced to Nancy that she was going on stage to help her cousin. Nancy held her friend's arm. "Please stay here. I'm sure all this is a hoax. Don't you remember that Mrs. Richards said there was a big surprise during the performance?"

George sat down again. "I guess you're right, Nancy."

By this time the magician was clapping his hands loudly to restore order on the stage. Over a microphone he announced, "This is all a hoax. Every missing article will be returned to its rightful owner at the end of the show. Please come back here afterward to get your property."

Members of the audience who had gathered around him acknowledged that they had come on stage out of curiosity and would wait to claim their property. They filed back to their seats.

"For a few minutes I was scared," Bess told Nancy, George, and Aunt Eloise. "Do you think they really mean what they say and will return our things?"

Nancy nodded. "I'm sure they will. If they hadn't been doing it in other shows, people would have notified the police."

Aunt Eloise added, "There has been no bad publicity or I would have heard about it."

Bess agreed, and her flushed face returned to the attractive pink and white it usually was.

When the show was over, George said to her, "Be sure to check your handbag and see that everything is still in it."

Bess caught her breath. "It's jammed with stuff. I hope I can remember what was there. Let me see: my wallet, credit cards, a little jewel bag with a bracelet and earrings. Perfume. My savings book. A letter from Dorothy Cross, the girl I met during my vacation in Maine. And, oh . . . yes."

"What?" George asked.

Bess lowered her eyes. "A picture of Dave."

Nancy smiled. "You wouldn't want to lose that for a million dollars, would you?"

"No, I wouldn't," Bess replied.

Dave Evans was a special friend of hers, and she knew that both Nancy and George carried photographs of their boyfriends, too. Nancy's purse contained a snapshot of Ned Nickerson in his football uniform, and George had Burt Eddleton's picture tucked in her wallet.

Bess hurried up to the stage with other members of the audience to claim her property. They were ushered into a back room. As people retrieved their possessions, they were asked to sign releases that read,

> I relieve the Hoaxters of any wrongdoing
> in playing a hoax on me.

"This is just a protection for us. We don't want to be accused later of not returning everything to you," the magician explained.

Bess found that the contents of her handbag were intact and signed the paper. Then she joined her friends and they left the theater with Aunt Eloise.

"That was quite an experience," Miss Drew remarked. "Annabella was right about a big surprise in the performance."

14

Nancy said nothing, but her mind was working fast. Why was it necessary for the Hoaxters to keep people's property for such a long time? They could have returned it at once. She began to feel suspicious about the troupe, but had nothing definite to go on.

As the girls prepared for bed, George yawned. "If the rest of the mystery is going to be filled with days like this one, we'll have plenty of excitement." The others agreed and said good night.

Directly after breakfast the following morning Bess received a phone call. A man who introduced himself as Howie Barker said, "I contacted your home in River Heights. Your mother told me where you were staying. I'd like very much to come and see you."

"I don't understand," Bess replied. "I've never met you."

"No, you haven't," Mr. Barker admitted. "But your mother felt that you might be interested in an offer I have for you. The company I represent is building a wonderful new seaside hotel. If you avail yourself of this opportunity, you will have perpetual low rates for yourself, your family and friends, and will get reservations anytime you choose to come."

"I don't know what to say," Bess told him. "My friends and I have plans for the day. Maybe some other time—"

Nancy and George stood close to Bess and had overheard the conversation. Nancy whispered, "Let him come!"

Bess looked surprised, but said to the stranger, "Well, all right. Can you make it right away?"

"I'll be there in half an hour," Mr. Barker said.

After Bess had hung up, she turned to Nancy. "Why did you want him to see us?"

Nancy told her that the scheme sounded like another swindle. "This Mr. Barker could be the man who sold Mrs. Richards the ticket for the fake world trip!"

"If that is so, then he might know we're on the case—" George began.

"And means to kidnap us?" Bess panicked.

"C'mon, Bess," Nancy said. "How could he possibly know of our connection with Mrs. Richards? I'd say he picked your name from some mailing list. You get more junk mail than anybody else I know. It's all coincidental, I'm sure."

George spoke up. "Why don't we ask Mrs. Richards to come over? If she can identify Barker as Henry Clark, we'll call the police and have him arrested!"

Aunt Eloise phoned her friend. The housekeeper answered and said Mrs. Richards was out and would not return until evening.

"That's too bad," Bess remarked.

16

Nancy said, "I have an idea how we might find out if Mr. Barker is the travel agent. Take his picture. Aunt Eloise, you have a camera, don't you?"

Miss Drew said, "Yes, and I happen to have fast film in it so we won't need a flash. Besides, the camera makes no noise when the shutter clicks. It'll be perfect for this purpose."

"Does it develop the picture instantly?" George asked.

"Yes. As soon as Annabella arrives home, you can show it to her."

As the time neared for Howie Barker's arrival, Bess became nervous. "I don't want to get mixed up in any kind of racket," she declared. "What am I supposed to tell him?"

"I'll stay in the room with you," George offered. "We'll figure out something."

It was decided that Nancy would hide and take the caller's picture while Bess and George kept him in animated conversation. Aunt Eloise could not wait for the stranger to arrive because she had classes at school. Before leaving, she warned the girls to be careful of any tricks the caller might play.

"I'm not going to let him hoax me!" Bess spoke up belligerently.

George added, "If you start to fall for any scheme, I'll take over."

Soon the house phone rang. Bess answered. The doorman announced that Mr. Howie Barker was there to see Miss Bess Marvin.

"Let him come up," Bess said, her voice betraying her slight nervousness.

Barker proved to be a good-looking, blond-haired man with gray at the temples, and a full blond-gray beard. The description was not like that of Henry Clark. The man was a glib talker. Bess ushered him into the living room, where Nancy was concealed behind a wall screen. She took several pictures when he walked in and others when he sat down on the couch.

"You girls will love this place," Howie Barker said, taking a large architect's drawing out of his briefcase. He spread it on the coffee table and with his pen pointed to the fine features of the place.

"Notice the little verandas off each bedroom. If you don't feel like going to the beach, you can sun yourself right there. If you don't want to go to the dining room, you can eat your meals out there, too."

George spoke up. "It's certainly a huge place. Where is it being built?"

Mr. Barker produced a brochure from his briefcase. It described the location as a secluded area of oceanfront in Maine.

"It has luxury as well as seclusion," he went on.

18

"I'm telling you, this is really an opportunity of a lifetime."

"Why did you pick my cousin for this offer?" George inquired.

"We have been approaching all the people who vacationed at the Silverline Hotel in Maine last season," Barker explained. "You see, the Silverline is owned by the same company, and we know their clientele would enjoy this kind of setup."

"What does it cost?" Bess asked.

"Only a thousand dollars. For that, you have guaranteed discount rates forever, much less than the regular price for a room."

"For a thousand dollars, you can spend a long time in a hotel," George pointed out.

"Not really," Barker objected. "Also, remember, your rates are guaranteed never to increase. Everything else goes up year after year. Right?"

Bess agreed. She was quite impressed with the proposal, but George thought of Nancy. Had she been able to take pictures of the man from every angle? Impatiently the girl looked at her wristwatch. Barker had been there twenty minutes, surely time enough to be photographed extensively.

Bess was about to say that she would try to get the money to avail herself of the offer, when she remembered Nancy's warning that this might be another swindle similar to Mrs. Richards's experience. She hesitated, then said, "The whole thing sounds wonderful. I'll tell you what I'll do. I'll contact a few people and let you know if I can borrow the money."

"Oh, that won't be necessary. Your mother told me you had your own savings account, and can spend the money as you wish."

"That's partly true, but I must think about your offer. Where can I find you?"

George fully expected the man not to give his address, but to her amazement he pulled a business card from his pocket and handed it to Bess.

"My phone number is on here," he said. "Be sure to let me know tomorrow." He stood up and shook hands with both girls, then they ushered him out of the apartment.

After George had closed the door, she smiled at her cousin. "Bess, I'm proud of you. For a moment I thought you'd fall for his scheme, but you handled it beautifully."

"It really sounds great," Bess countered as they entered the living room again. Nancy stepped from her hiding place, and the girls asked her if she had taken good pictures.

"Oh, yes, several," Nancy replied. "I'm sorry I didn't have a tape recorder to get the whole conversation. By the way, I don't think we should wait for Mrs. Richards to come home. Let's go to the police at once with these photographs and the card Mr. Barker gave Bess. We'll tell them our suspicions."

"How did the pictures come out?" George asked. Nancy showed them to her friends. They were excellent and the young detective felt sure that if the police had a record of the man, they could identify him easily.

The three sleuths quickly left the apartment and headed for the nearest police station. When they walked in, Nancy asked if it were possible to talk to the chief privately.

The desk sergeant asked the girls' names and the nature of their business. Nancy introduced her friends and herself and added, "I think we have a lead on a con man."

The sergeant looked at her in surprise, but made no further comment. He picked up his phone and dialed the chief's number.

After a short conversation, he said to Nancy, "Chief Raleigh will see you. Walk down the corridor and take the first turn to your left. Watch for the sign on the door."

In a few minutes the young detective and her friends were standing before the chief. He was a ruddy-faced man who reminded them of Police Chief McGinnis in River Heights.

"I understand you have some interesting information for me," the officer said, smiling.

21

Nancy nodded and took Barker's pictures from her handbag. Bess produced the man's business card.

"Have you any record of this person?" Nancy inquired.

The chief called in a deputy and asked him to look in the files. While waiting for an answer, Nancy told Chief Raleigh about the mysterious caller and the proposition he had offered Bess.

The officer frowned. "It certainly sounds like a swindle."

When the deputy returned, he said they had no picture of a suspect resembling the man in Nancy's photographs. The deputy had rubbed out the beard. Still the face did not resemble anyone in their file. Also, the name Howie Barker had not been reported in connection with any crime.

Nancy thanked the chief, who promised to investigate anyway. She left two of the photographs and the calling card with him as well as Aunt Eloise's address and phone number.

"We'll let you know if anything turns up," he promised.

On the way outside the building, Nancy said she hoped Mrs. Richards would return sooner than expected. She was eager to show her the photographs. "And there's something else I can't get out of my mind," she added.

"What is it?" Bess asked.

# 3

## *Poison!*

Bess and George asked Nancy to tell them what was bothering her.

"How Howie Barker got your name and home address. I don't believe his story about having the list of guests of the Silverline Hotel. Bess, will you phone your mother and verify his story?"

When they reached Aunt Eloise's apartment, Bess called Mrs. Marvin.

"Oh, Bess, you didn't get into any trouble because I gave Miss Drew's address to Mr. Barker, did you?"

"No, but he tried to sell me a lifetime reservation in a new hotel. Did you tell him about my savings account?"

"No!" Mrs. Marvin exclaimed.

Bess cried out, "He claims you said I could spend it any way I wished!"

"That's not true."

"Nancy thinks he's a con man, and we've reported him to the police."

"Good."

When Bess repeated her mother's denial, Nancy bobbed her head. "I suspected that. I'll bet he was told about your savings book after the Hoaxters examined your handbag. And he knew about your vacation in Maine because they read Dorothy Cross's letter!"

The girls walked along the street silently for a while, then Nancy said, "I wish Mrs. Richards were home. I'd like to find out if Barker was her travel agent."

"Perhaps she returned earlier than her house-keeper expected," Bess suggested. "Why don't we call her?"

"Good idea," Nancy agreed and did so.

The girls were in luck. Mrs. Richards answered personally and invited them to come at once.

When they arrived, she ushered them into her living room. It was beautifully furnished in French Provincial decor with lovely statues and paintings.

"I'm delighted to see you," she said. "Do you have a clue yet in my case?"

"Perhaps," Nancy said. She told the woman about Bess's caller and showed her the photographs. "Is this the man who swindled you?"

Mrs. Richards studied the pictures intently. "No, I think not. Mr. Clark had a dark beard."

Nancy told her of Barker's offer to Bess, and Mrs. Richards frowned. "He certainly sounds like the man who came to see me. A glib talker and very personable."

Nancy nodded. "Have you heard anything more from him?"

"No," Mrs. Richards replied. "But lately I've had a ton of mail. It's mostly requests from charitable organizations, but there are two letters that might interest you. I'll get them."

She went into another room and returned a few moments later, handing Nancy two envelopes. One letter, neatly typed on very expensive stationery, was from a man who offered copies of rare paintings at ridiculous prices. He guaranteed that they were very special and a once-in-a-lifetime bargain. The letter read:

Fool your friends. They couldn't tell the difference between the copy and the real thing!

George wrinkled her forehead. "That sounds like a con game!"

The others agreed. Nancy unfolded the second letter. It advertised a fine collection of old coins. The "bargains" were so cheap that the deal definitely sounded like a hoax.

"May I take the two ads with me?" Nancy requested.

"Certainly," Mrs. Richards replied. "I have no intention of following them up. I've been hurt once. That's enough."

Nancy put the letters into her handbag. "I'll try to find out more about these offers," she said.

"Mrs. Richards, you have a fascinating apartment," Bess commented. "Did you collect all the works of art in this room?"

"A great many of them, yes. Others were gifts to me. Would you like to see the rest of my home?"

"Oh, yes," the girls chorused.

As they were led from room to room, the young detectives realized that each was furnished in the style of a foreign country, including a Japanese room which Bess liked most.

"I don't care for it myself," George remarked under her breath. "I wouldn't want to kneel down every time I looked into the mirror of my dressing table!"

The others laughed.

"Japanese girls think nothing of it," Mrs. Richards said.

She slid aside a panel in the wall and pulled out a tufted silk comforter with gaily painted figures of dancing girls on it. She spread the puff on the floor and announced that this was a typical Japanese mattress.

"Personally I think that's why their women have such straight backs," she said.

"Don't they use a pillow?" Bess asked.

Their hostess answered by producing another item from the closet. It was cylinder-shaped, about six inches in diameter and covered with black material.

"This is very heavy because the pillow is filled with sand," Mrs. Richards explained.

"That's a pillow?" Bess asked in disbelief.

"Yes. However, many Japanese have adopted our Western ways and use beds, mattresses and somewhat softer pillows now."

Bess giggled. "They're smart."

"The reason Japanese women years ago needed to sleep on this type of pillow is rather interesting," Mrs. Richards went on. "Having their full-length hair professionally set was a long, costly process. To keep their hairdos intact between washings, the women slept with their necks against the hard pillows."

George grinned. "I'm glad I don't have to worry about that sort of thing," she said and shook her short, plainly combed hair.

Mrs. Richards led the girls through other rooms. Heavy silken drapes ornamented the windows and Oriental rugs lay on the floors.

The last room they came to was decorated in Florentine style. Everything was ornate, from the heavily carved furniture to the slatted, painted wooden blinds. In one corner stood a mannequin dressed in a Florentine soldier's uniform.

George remarked, "He looks pretty fancy for someone going into battle."

Mrs. Richards smiled. "I doubt that anyone wearing an outfit like this did much fighting. It probably belonged to a general."

Nancy walked closer to the figure and surveyed it from all angles. Suddenly she noticed a partially concealed pocket with a slight bulge. She put her hand inside and felt a small object.

"Something's in this pocket," she said to Mrs. Richards.

"Really?" the woman asked. "I didn't know that. Let's see what it is."

Nancy pulled out a small glass vial with a gold filigree covering. Mrs. Richards read an Italian inscription on the bottom. A startled look came over her face.

"Where in the world did this come from? I never saw it before!"

"Perhaps the vial was in the uniform for centu-

ries and no one ever noticed it," George suggested. "Does it contain anything?"

"A deadly poison!" Mrs. Richards replied.

Bess shivered. "Did the soldier carry it to use on an enemy?"

Mrs. Richards shook her head. "In the days when Florentine intrigue was at its height, nearly every member of the army carried a vial of poison in case he was captured. Rather than go to prison or be tortured, he would kill himself."

"Ugh!" Bess said. "That's terrible."

The others did not comment, but Nancy suggested they take the vial to a medical laboratory for testing. "We should find out if it's still potent," she said.

"There's a medical lab not far from here," Mrs. Richards said. "I've known the owner for years."

Since the lab was located nearby, she and the girls walked over. On the way, Nancy asked Mrs. Richards if she had had any news about Roscoe and her car.

"Oh, yes. He had a very trying adventure. He was parked not far from the terminal waiting for us, when suddenly two men jumped into the back seat. They ordered Roscoe to take them to a certain address. When he told them his car was not a taxi and they must get out, the men refused. One said Roscoe would be harmed if he did not follow their orders."

"Poor Roscoe!" Bess exclaimed.

Mrs. Richards went on. "There was nothing he could do, so he started for the place the men indicated. But they never got there."

"What happened?" George wanted to know.

"They told him suddenly to stop and get out of the car. Then one of the men jumped behind the wheel and drove away. Roscoe yelled at them but they paid no attention. The police never did locate my stolen car, and poor Roscoe was a wreck after he hiked back to town."

"That's a shame," Nancy said sympathetically.

"Roscoe blamed himself," Mrs. Richards went on. "But I told him it was not his fault. The insurance company is going to settle if my automobile is not found within a certain time period, and we're looking at a new car."

Nancy asked if Roscoe had heard the men say anything that might lead to their arrest.

"I don't know if there's any significance to this," the woman replied, "but one of them said, 'This is a good hoax on that rich widow.' Then the two of them laughed uproariously."

By this time the group had reached the medical laboratory. Mrs. Richards told Mr. Horner, the owner, that her young visitors had found the vial in an old costume and wondered if the poison were still effective.

Mr. Horner asked his assistant, whose name was

31

Enzo Scorpio, to take the vial into the lab and test it. Five minutes later the young man returned, confirming that it was potent.

"What kind of poison is it?" Mrs. Richards asked.

"It's extracted from poisonous mushrooms," the technician replied.

"In that case," Mr. Horner said, "the vial is more valuable than its contents. I believe it was made by an artisan in the fifteenth century. It's absolutely airtight. That's why the poison has not evaporated. As a matter of fact, if you would like to sell the vial, I'd be glad to buy it. I know a man who collects this kind of thing."

Mrs. Richards hesitated. Nancy felt sure that she was about to agree and grabbed the woman's hand, squeezing it tightly.

Mrs. Richards understood. "I don't want to sell it," she replied.

"I can't blame you," he said with a smile. "If you'd like to find out if it's genuine Florentine, I recommend you take it to a specialist on fifteenth-century artwork. The best man I know is at the Metro Museum in Washington, D.C."

Mrs. Richards's eyebrows shot up. "Oh? That's a good idea. I'm planning to visit a friend in Washington. . . . I'm flying out tomorrow morning on the shuttle. I'll certainly look up that man."

Mr. Horner wrote the specialist's name and address on a piece of paper, and handed it to Mrs. Richards. Then the group left the laboratory.

Nancy, Bess, and George returned to Aunt Eloise's apartment. Again they read the two advertisements that Nancy had brought from Mrs. Richards.

George said, "Would it be a good idea for you to contact these places and wire the money?"

"If we do that," Nancy said, "I'm afraid we'll never hear from them, and our money will be gone. But here's an idea. How about suggesting your scheme to the police to get evidence?"

"To do what?" George asked.

"Have a detective write from his home to the two companies and include checks that will bounce. When they're returned, the police can see where the con men tried to cash them. They can contact the companies' banks at once to find out more about the men and maybe get their addresses. One of the persons might be Howie Barker!"

George grinned. "Rubber checks! It's a terrific idea."

Nancy telephoned the chief who said the plan might work.

"Good thinking," he added. "Thank you."

When Aunt Eloise returned, she and the girls had

dinner. Then George said, "Let's see another Hoaxter magic show. This time *I'd* like to be a volunteer and go up on stage to watch their tricks."

"I hope you learn more than I did," Bess said.

When the moment arrived for people in the audience to join the artists on stage, George hurried forward and leaped up the steps. She was the first onlooker to arrive, but the sleight of hand man ignored her and selected ten other people.

"Sorry," he said to the rest. "That's all we can take."

"But I was here first!" George objected. "I should have—"

The magician looked at her stonily. "Young lady, I'm sorry. Please return to your seat."

George was tempted to argue further with the man, but he was already talking to someone else. Angrily she left the stage, wondering why he would not let her stay!

# 4

## Airport Theft

When George returned to her seat, Nancy, Bess, and Aunt Eloise immediately asked her what had happened.

"The sleight of hand man wouldn't let me watch the performance," George replied.

"Why not?" Bess demanded.

George shrugged. "Maybe I'm not his type!"

Nancy frowned. "It's my guess the Hoaxters know we're amateur detectives and don't want any of us close enough to see their tricks."

"It's possible," George replied. "But I wonder how they found out who we are."

Next morning after breakfast Nancy called Mrs. Richards to ask if she had heard any more about the travel agent who had swindled her. Trudie, the housekeeper, answered and said that Mrs. Richards had already left for Washington.

"Do you know if she had any news from the police?" Nancy asked.

"No, she hasn't," Trudie replied. "However, a man phoned yesterday afternoon and asked for you."

"For me?" Nancy was surprised. "What was his name?"

"He didn't tell me. He said he had a gift to deliver to Nancy Drew and asked if you were living here. Also what kind of work you do."

"What did you tell him?" Nancy asked.

"The truth," Trudie replied. "I didn't see any reason not to. I said you and your friends were staying with your Aunt Eloise and that you were amateur detectives."

Nancy caught her breath. She was disappointed that Trudie had given out this information.

"I told the man if he wanted to leave the present here I would see that you received it," the housekeeper added.

Despite the fact that Nancy considered the matter most unfortunate, she remained calm. "Thank you very much," she said. "When the package arrives, let me know."

Nancy hung up and repeated the conversation

36

to her friends. "I'm sure there's no gift involved," she declared. "Somehow the caller found out that we know Mrs. Richards, and he used the present as an excuse to inquire who we are."

"Do you think he's the same man who fleeced Mrs. Richards?" Bess asked.

"It's possible," Nancy replied.

"So he's either a member of the Hoaxters or connected with them," George put in. "That's why they wouldn't let me stay on stage last night!"

"I don't believe he's a member of the troupe," Bess argued. "He's more likely a con man. We'd better watch our step."

George said, "What about Howie Barker?"

"None of the Hoaxters, according to the program, is called Barker," Nancy explained. "But it could be an assumed name. And the performers are so made up during the show, we wouldn't necessarily recognize him."

She was thoughtful for a few moments, then added, "Why don't we go to the matinee today and do some real sleuthing?"

"Good idea," George agreed.

Bess asked, "How can we? They'll remember us and most likely won't let *you* on stage either."

Nancy smiled. "I wouldn't walk up from the audience. I'd rather try to slip in backstage. Perhaps I'll find a clue there."

As soon the group had had lunch, they taxied to the theater. As the cab pulled up, all of them were amazed to find the building deserted.

Nancy said to the taxi driver, "Do you know whether the performance has been cancelled?"

"I heard," he replied, "that the show closed. The Hoaxters moved out bag and baggage."

"That's amazing," George remarked. "We were here last night and no announcement was made."

Nancy asked the man if he had any idea where the troupe had gone. He shook his head. "Do you want me to take you home again?"

Nancy decided to stay. She paid the driver and the girls got out.

"What's on your mind?" Bess asked Nancy.

"I'd like to find out where the magicians went. I suggest we question restaurant and store owners in the neighborhood."

The group divided. Bess and George began to inquire at shops, while Nancy checked the various eating places. When she walked into a luncheonette across the street, the hostess approached her and asked where she would like to be seated.

Nancy smiled. "Thank you, but I don't plan to stay. I was wondering if you could give me any information about the Hoaxters who left so suddenly last night. Have you any idea where they went?"

The hostess shook her head. "I'll ask the waitresses. Maybe one of them knows."

She went to the kitchen and returned a few minutes later with a pretty girl. "Susie, this young lady is trying to locate the Hoaxters. You say two of the magicians at dinner last night were talking about leaving."

Susie nodded and giggled. "One of them gave me an extra large tip and said, 'Here's something for you to remember me by.'"

The waitress said she had expressed regret at his leaving and asked where he was going. "He whispered in my ear, 'Don't tell anybody, but our next stop is Mexico City.'"

Nancy smiled. "I'm glad you *did* tell us, Susie."

The girl giggled again. "Oh, I'm sure he was only kidding about keeping it a secret, like I was kidding when I told him I'd miss him. I won't miss him, only his tips! He always gave me more than anyone else."

Nancy thanked Susie and the hostess and was about to leave when she noticed several luscious-looking cakes displayed on a glass counter near the door.

"Shall I take one?" Nancy asked herself. "Mm, I can't resist. They look delicious."

She bought a lemon layer cake, then walked out of the luncheonette. When she reached the theater where she was to meet Bess and George, the girls were not there. They arrived about ten minutes later.

Bess's eyes went immediately to the cake box in Nancy's hand. "Is there something rich and fattening inside?" She beamed.

"And it's not for you!" her cousin replied quickly.

"Why, George Fayne, as if I—"

"I've had terrific luck." Nancy interrupted the friendly squabble. "You'd never guess where the Hoaxters have gone."

"Where?" Bess asked eagerly.

"Mexico City!"

George lifted her eyebrows. "If they skipped town, they sure made a big jump!"

The others agreed. All felt that the troupe's sudden departure had not been planned.

"Do you suppose it was because of us?"

"I wonder," Nancy replied.

The group hailed another taxi and went back to the apartment. When they entered, the telephone was ringing. Nancy dashed to answer it.

"Oh, Nancy, I've been trying for hours to get you!" It was Mrs. Richards. She was hysterical.

"What's the matter?" Nancy asked.

"I'm beside myself! My vial of poison has been stolen!"

40

"When?"

"It must have happened at the airport in New York this morning. I had a long wait before my flight and dozed off in the lounge."

"Oh, dear," Nancy said. "Where are you now?"

"At my friend's apartment in Washington. Her name is Mrs. Marian Greening. Better take her phone number down in case you want to reach me." She gave the number, then said, "Oh, Nancy, what am I going to do? Not only is the vial valuable, but whoever stole it might not realize it contains poison and may harm himself or someone else!"

Mrs. Richards began to sob uncontrollably. Suddenly she gasped for breath.

"Mrs. Richards!" Nancy called out. "Mrs. Richards, are you all right?"

There was no reply, but Nancy heard a scraping noise. Then a man's voice sounded over the phone. "Don't worry," he said. "I'll take care of her."

The next moment the phone clicked. The man had hung up!

# 5

## *A Planned Accident*

Nancy frowned. "That's strange," she muttered.

"What is?" Bess asked. She and George had rushed to their friend's side and wanted to know what had happened.

Nancy repeated her conversation with Mrs. Richards, saying the last thing she had heard from the woman was a gasp. "Then a man told me he would take care of her and hung up."

"Try calling back," George suggested. "He could have been her friend's husband."

Nancy dialed the number Mrs. Richards had given her. No one answered.

"Maybe the man took her to the doctor," Bess suggested.

"I don't know," Nancy said. "I'll ask the police to check on her."

She contacted the authorities in Washington and was connected with a captain. Quickly she explained the matter. "Could you send someone to Mrs. Greening's apartment to see that Mrs. Richards is all right?" she requested.

"Sure will," the officer said. "Please give me your name and number. I'll call you back."

A few minutes later the phone rang. Nancy answered. To her surprise, it was the Washington police.

"You've seen our friend already?" she asked, incredulous.

"No. I'm double-checking your story. We get so many prank calls, that whenever possible we confirm a complaint before sending someone out. An officer will drive to Mrs. Greening's apartment now. You'll hear from us soon."

Nancy and her friends paced about the living room restlessly, wondering what was happening in Washington. Finally the young sleuth could stand it no longer. She dialed Mrs. Greening's number. A policeman answered.

"This is Nancy Drew," she said. "I'm so glad you got there. Did you find Mrs. Richards?"

"Yes. She's right here. Apparently she fainted while speaking to you."

43

"But a man picked up the phone and said he would take care of her," Nancy pointed out. "Who was he?"

"A deliveryman who was putting food into the refrigerator while Mrs. Richards was talking to you."

"Oh? But I called back right after he hung up, and there was no answer."

"After Mrs. Richards fainted, he put her on the couch, then rushed down to Dr. Marsiono who has his practice on the first floor. Luckily the doctor was in and could come up. He revived Mrs. Richards. She's all right now."

"May I speak to her, please?" Nancy requested.

"One minute," the officer said and handed the receiver to the woman.

Mrs. Richards was still upset about the theft. "I suppose I got so worked up that I passed out while I was talking to you," she told Nancy.

"Will you be all right?" the girl asked, worried.

"Oh, sure. My friend will be home soon—as a matter of fact, here she comes now. What a surprise she'll have, finding the police here! Well, my dear, thank you for your help."

The following morning Chief Raleigh from the New York police asked the girls to come to headquarters. "We have news about the man Nancy Drew photographed," he said.

Nancy promised to go at once. Aunt Eloise had already left for school. Bess and George accompanied the young detective.

When the girls walked out of the apartment building, they noticed a car parked not far from the entrance. The driver appeared to be sleeping since his head was bent low over the steering wheel.

"Funny place to take a nap," Bess commented.

Just then a taxi drove up and the girls signaled for it to stop. They climbed in and Nancy gave the driver directions. He looked at her quizzically, but she volunteered no further information about their errand.

George noticed that the driver in the parked car had suddenly started his engine and was following the taxi. She wondered if this was on purpose.

Presently he drove up close behind them, then pulled out as if to pass. Instead, he deliberately sideswiped the taxi, whose right front wheel jumped the curb.

"Oh!" Bess cried out. She tumbled off the rear seat and hit her head.

Nancy, on the left side, got the full impact of the crash. Instinctively she braced herself on the backrest of the driver's seat and escaped injury. George managed to avoid getting hurt, but like Nancy, she was badly shaken.

With trembling hands they pulled Bess up to the seat. "Are you all right?" Nancy asked worriedly.

"I—I guess so. My head hurts where I bumped it, though."

"That man hit us on purpose!" Nancy declared angrily.

She looked out the window just in time to see their attacker rounding the next corner. Apparently there had not been enough damage to his car to disable it.

"Did you get his license number?" Bess asked hopefully.

"Yes," Nancy replied. "Luckily he was still close enough when I looked out."

George pointed to their driver, who was slumped over the steering wheel. He did not move and the engine was not running. Apparently it had stalled from the impact.

"He must be unconscious!" George exclaimed.

She jumped from the cab, opened the right front door, and slid across the seat. She tried to revive the driver but without success. Quickly she picked up the radiophone and called the taxi company. While waiting for a reply, she looked for the cab's license that was posted on the dashboard.

"Hello," she said after a man answered her call. "This is cab 52341. We were rammed deliberately by another car and Max Topping, the driver, is unconscious. Could you please notify the police and send an ambulance for him?"

The dispatcher promised to do so at once. A few minutes later the police arrived. Nancy gave them the license number of the car that sideswiped them and told the police what had happened.

Just then the ambulance pulled alongside the cab. Two men put the stricken driver on a stretcher, then carefully transferred him into their vehicle. Seconds later they were on their way to the hospital.

The police officers asked the girls where they were headed. When the men learned it was police headquarters, they offered to take them there.

In Chief Raleigh's office, a stenographer recorded Nancy's story. The young sleuth gave the details of the accident and signed the transcript. Shortly afterward a report came in saying the car which rammed the taxi had been stolen and was abandoned.

"That's unfortunate," the officer said. "We found only the owner's fingerprints on the steering wheel, so the thief must have worn gloves. Obviously the accident was planned because there was only minimal damage to the side of the car. The driver either had a grudge against the cabbie or you girls. Can you shed any light on the matter?"

"As I told you before, we suspect Howie Barker

to be a con man. But we haven't found any new clues."

The chief smiled. "We have, however. That's why I wanted you to come down. We received a new picture in the rogues' gallery that matches the photograph you've taken, Nancy. His full beard is one of his many disguises. The man is listed by the name of Ralph Rafferty. Originally he worked for the Francisco Insurance Company. He proved to be dishonest and went to prison for forgery."

"But now he's free?" Nancy asked.

"Yes. After being released from prison, Rafferty disappeared from the West Coast. He swindled someone out of a large sum of money in Chicago and is wanted again. Your clue will help us a great deal."

"Did you check the telephone number and address on his calling card?" Nancy asked.

"Yes. It was an apartment here in the city, but he moved out before we got there. We questioned the superintendent and other tenants, but no one knew anything about him. He was a resident only a short time. But we think he's still in this area."

"I'm not sure about that," Nancy said. "We suspect that he may be in cahoots with a group of performers called the Hoaxters. They left unexpectedly for Mexico City."

The officer's eyebrows shot up. "Oh? That's

interesting. I'll get in touch with the police there and ask them to be on the lookout for Rafferty, alias Barker."

"I certainly hope they catch him," Bess said. "He came near getting some money from me. He's a slick talker."

"And a very good-looking and likeable person," George added. "I guess it's easy for him to sell phony products."

"I'm afraid so," the chief agreed. "Thank you very much, girls."

He opened his desk drawer and handed Nancy the original snapshots she had taken. "We've made duplicates of these," he said.

When the girls left headquarters, Nancy suggested they go directly to Aunt Eloise's apartment and do no more sleuthing for the day.

"All I want to do is lie in a tub of hot water. I'm stiff all over," she confessed.

"And I'd like to go to sleep," George said. She still felt shaky from the accident.

Bess nodded. She had a terrible headache. Quickly Nancy hailed a cab and the girls climbed in. When they reached the apartment, she phoned the taxi company to find out how their driver was. The answer was a relief: he had suffered a slight concussion, but would be all right in a couple of days.

When Aunt Eloise returned from school later that afternoon, she was amazed by her visitors' story.

"You're lucky not to have been seriously injured," she said. "Did you get a good look at the man who ran into you?"

"Only a fleeting glimpse," George said. "Not enough to identify him."

They tried to figure out who the attacker could have been. Nancy said she had a strong hunch he was connected with the Hoaxters.

Aunt Eloise was inclined to agree. "But why did he want to harm you?" she asked.

There was silence for a few minutes, then Nancy said, "I think we should go to Mexico City and continue our sleuthing. We shouldn't let the Hoaxters get away from us!"

"You're right," Aunt Eloise said. "How I wish that I could go with you! But of course, that's impossible."

Bess and George felt Nancy's suggestion was a good one. George added with a sigh, however, "I'll have to phone home and try to get more money. Frankly, my detective allowance account is down to zero!"

# 6

## Clue to a Suspect

Bess was the first to call her parents. While the other girls waited eagerly, she explained their plans and said she would like to join Nancy on her trip to Mexico. The Marvins readily agreed.

George phoned next, but she had a more difficult time getting permission. Mr. Fayne reminded his daughter that she had, indeed, used up her detective allowance.

"But Dad, this is *very* important!" George pleaded. "Would you lend me the money and after I get home, I'll earn some and pay you back?"

Mr. Fayne chuckled. "You're working hard now. How would it be if you got paid for being a detective?"

"No, Dad. If I accept money for my work, it would take me out of the amateur class. And I know Mr. Drew wouldn't like that. Besides, I couldn't work with Nancy and Bess any longer."

"Okay, you've convinced me," Mr. Fayne said fondly. He promised to raise her allowance to pay for the trip. "But be sure you solve the mystery!" he teased.

George laughed. "With Nancy carrying the ball we won't fail."

As soon as the girls had finished their calls, Nancy contacted her father and told him about the proposed trip to Mexico City. Then she phoned Mrs. Richards. Nancy was glad to learn that the woman was feeling fine, and revealed their plans. She asked Mrs. Richards, however, to keep their trip a secret.

"Of course I will," the woman promised. "But I think you should tell me where you're staying in case I need to reach you."

"At the Fortunato Hotel," Nancy replied. "We'll let you know what's happening."

She made reservations on a flight for early the next morning. After breakfast, they said good-by to Aunt Eloise.

"And thank you for your wonderful hospitality," Bess added.

The girls arrived in Mexico City during the

afternoon. While claiming their baggage, the three Americans heard nothing but Spanish spoken. Bess and George stared at each other. They did not understand a word!

"Nancy, I'm glad you speak Spanish," George said. "We'd have a hard time otherwise."

Nancy laughed. "You two should really learn the language. It isn't difficult."

The cousins made up their minds then and there that they would take lessons. Nancy was right. It was becoming more and more important for Americans to learn the language of their neighbors just across the Rio Grande River.

The girls took a cab to the Fortunato. When they walked up to the desk, Nancy said to the clerk, "We'd like a large room for the three of us."

"Your names, please?"

"Nancy Drew, Bess Marvin, and George Fayne."

"Nancy Drew?" The clerk stared at her. "Please wait a minute," he said. "The manager has a message for you." He turned and hurried into a back office.

Nancy looked at her friends. "I wonder what this is all about?" she said. "Not many people knew we'd be here and the ones who did promised to keep it a secret."

A good-looking Mexican in a white suit came from the rear room and addressed Nancy. "I will

53

have to ask you to come into my office. There is something I must discuss with you."

The girls followed him and he motioned them to be seated in his small, paneled room. The girls were worried. Was bad news from home awaiting them?

The manager, who introduced himself as Señor Gonzales, said, "I am sorry to detain you, but the police telephoned and asked me to do so."

Nancy frowned. "How do the police know we are here?"

"They alerted every hotel in town," Señor Gonzales revealed. "We have your reservation."

The conversation had been in Spanish, and Nancy turned to translate for her friends. When Señor Gonzales realized Bess and George did not speak his language, he switched to English.

"The clerk told me you were here and I called Lieutenant Tara. He should be here any minute. Please be patient."

The girls looked at one another in dismay. Members of their families and Mrs. Richards were the only people who could have phoned! Just then the officer walked into the room. Fortunately he spoke English so that Bess and George could follow the conversation.

"I understand that you are detectives," Lieutenant Tara said.

54

Nancy replied, "I guess you might call us that. Why?"

"I have been told that you are practicing without a license."

"License!" Nancy protested. "We're strictly amateurs and never get paid for our work."

Lieutenant Tara's eyebrows shot up. "Can you prove it?"

The girls were stymied for a moment. They were in a foreign country! How could they possibly prove that they never charged for their detective services?

Finally Nancy said, "We have no proof with us. But if you phone my father in River Heights in the United States, he'll back up our statement. He's a lawyer. And you might phone Chief McGinnis of the River Heights police force. He has known me ever since I was a little girl."

The officer rubbed his chin. "Your father is an attorney?"

Bess answered, "Yes, and very well known!"

"We came to Mexico City to locate a con man who is wanted by the New York police," Nancy said.

"Amazing!" the manager said.

Lieutenant Tara picked up the phone and first called Mr. Drew, then Chief McGinnis. They confirmed the fact that the girls were strictly amateur detectives and Chief McGinnis said, "Nancy Drew is the daughter of a famous attorney and she is known for her talent in solving mysteries."

Lieutenant Tara thanked the chief and said good-by.

George spoke up. "Who gave you this false information about us?"

The officer hesitated. "I don't know. Our chief received the message. Why don't you ask him personally?"

Señor Gonzales offered to get the chief on the line. In a few moments Nancy was explaining to him the girls' mission in Mexico City.

He told her that the message had come from someone in the U.S. Department of Justice, but that he had not caught the man's name. He then asked Nancy if she and her friends had any more to tell.

"Indeed we have!" Nancy replied. "This is outrageous. We have never been investigated by the Department of Justice. Your anonymous caller gave you false information."

The chief cleared his throat, but did not comment. Instead, he asked to speak to Lieutenant Tara again. The chief told him that he saw no reason for detaining the girls and Tara should return to headquarters. When the officer finished, Tara smiled and relayed the message.

"Thank you," Nancy said. "That's a relief."

Bess grinned. "I feel a hundred pounds lighter!"

After Tara had left, Señor Gonzales apologized profusely to the girls. He told the desk clerk to give them a fine room with bath. "That may compensate for all the trouble we Mexicans have caused you." He smiled broadly.

The girls found the quarters delightful. While they were unpacking, the three friends talked about what had happened.

"I don't understand how the anonymous caller knew we were coming to Mexico City," Bess declared.

George said, "The Hoaxters left New York before we made our plans!"

"That's true," Nancy admitted. "Perhaps Howie Barker or another confederate stayed behind. He could have visited the luncheonette and learned from Susie the waitress that I had inquired where the Hoaxters had gone."

"I see what you mean," Bess said. "And after he found out we *knew* they went to Mexico City, he figured we would follow and warned the theatrical group."

"That's right. Then Barker called the police, pretending to work with the U.S. Department of Justice."

They had just finished unpacking when the telephone rang. Aunt Eloise Drew was calling. "I just heard from the New York police department," she told Nancy. "They have unearthed a clue to the thief who stole the vial of poison. His name is Enzo Scorpio."

"He's the assistant to Mr. Horner who owns the medical lab in New York!" Nancy exclaimed.

"That's correct," Aunt Eloise replied. "He's originally from Mexico City. The police think he may have returned there and advise you to keep your eyes open. You may be able to track him down."

"I wonder if he's trying to sell the vial," Nancy mused.

"It's likely that he'll approach a collector," Aunt Eloise said. "At least that's what Mr. Horner believes. He notified the police when Scorpio disappeared unexpectedly, taking all the cash in the lab with him."

After Nancy had hung up, Bess looked alarmed. "I hope that poison doesn't get into the hands of the con men. Can you imagine what would happen?"

Nancy nodded, then changed the subject. "What do you say we go see the Hoaxters?"

"Good idea," her friends agreed.

"I wonder if the show is the same here as it was in New York," George added.

The girls inquired at the desk where the magicians were scheduled to appear and learned that the theater was not far away. There was no matinee. The evening performance would start at eight o'clock.

Bess was worried that the girls would be recognized by the performers. "Why don't we disguise ourselves?" she suggested.

"How?" George asked.

"We could buy Mexican dresses, and shawls to wear on our heads. If anyone gets too close, we can just pull the shawls halfway up over our faces."

"Good idea," Nancy agreed, and the girls spent the rest of the afternoon shopping. They found an attractive boutique owned by Señora Clara.

"May I help you?" she asked in perfect English.

"What do you think of this one?" Nancy asked her companions. She was holding a pretty turquoise skirt in front of her.

"That is a beautiful choice," the proprietor remarked. "It matches your eyes so well."

"She's right, Nancy," Bess said. "If only I could find something to suit . . ."

"Your waist!" George laughed. "Señora, do you carry chubby sizes?"

Her cousin bristled. "Thanks a lot, George."

Señora Clara smiled. "You remind me so much of my favorite nieces in the States," she said. "I'm sure I can find something just right for all of you."

As promised, the young detectives were able to

select just what they wanted. When they arrived at the theater that evening in their attractive Mexican clothes and new hairdos, only a few minutes remained before curtain time.

The girls glanced at the program and noticed that the sleight of hand man was listed as Ronaldo Jensen, the same person they had seen previously.

Just before the performance started, a beautiful woman arrived and sat down in the aisle seat next to Nancy. She was expensively and tastefully dressed and carried a large beaded evening bag.

During intermission, she introduced herself to Nancy in Spanish as Señora Rosa Mendez, a lonely widow.

"My family lives in Oaxaca," she explained. "I have a darling little granddaughter named Dolores, but I don't see her very often because she lives too far away. I really miss her very much. I'll show you a picture of her."

The woman opened her purse and took out a snapshot of the little girl, who looked to be about nine years old.

"She's darling," said Nancy, gazing at the dark-haired, bright-eyed child. "I'm not surprised you'd like to see her more often. I'm sure the show will lighten your spirits," she added with a smile. "By the way, do you speak English?"

"Yes."

"Good," said Nancy. "My friends don't understand Spanish."

At the beginning of the second act, the Hoaxters performed a new trick. One of them raced down the center aisle, holding a flaming torch in his mouth. He crossed the rear of the theater and returned to the stage via a side aisle. Then he took the torch out of his mouth and extinguished the flames. The man opened his mouth wide to show that nothing inside had been burned.

"An amazing feat," Señora Mendez said to Nancy.

"Indeed it is," the girl agreed.

Just then the sleight of hand man appeared and invited members of the audience to come forward and watch how some of the tricks were done.

Señora Mendez said, "Oh, I'd love to see that!" Before Nancy could stop her, the woman left her seat and hurried down the aisle.

Bess whispered, "I hope she won't be approached by any of the con men later on. Señora Mendez looks as if she has plenty of money; just the kind of person they're after."

The show proceeded. Clever tricks were done by the magicians. The audience laughed and clapped. The people who had gone on stage had become so absorbed by the performance, none of them noticed that several of their watches, necklaces, wallets, and handbags had disappeared. The sleight of hand man assured them that all articles would be returned after the show.

"Please return to your seats," he requested.

Señora Mendez said to Nancy, "They took my handbag. Do you think they will really give it back to me?"

Nancy said she was sure they would, but added, "Did you have anything valuable in it?"

"Yes, I did," the woman replied. "My savings bankbook, some money, and several letters and papers that I would hate to have anyone else read."

"Do they contain something confidential?" Nancy asked, worried that the Hoaxters might take advantage of this.

"Yes," Señora Mendez answered. "There was important background information about my family that no outsider should know about!"

Nancy had a sudden hunch. She felt positive that such information could indeed be used to blackmail the woman!

# 7

## *Pyramid Chase*

In a loud whisper, Nancy said to the distraught woman, "I'm sure you'll get your handbag back. My friends and I saw two Hoaxter shows in New York, and Bess's handbag was taken. But it was returned afterward."

"Oh, good," Señora Mendez said and settled back in her seat to enjoy the balance of the performance. As soon as the show was over, however, she dashed down the aisle and up the steps to the stage.

"Do you have property you wish to claim?" the sleight of hand man asked her.

"Yes, I do. I want my handbag at once!"

"Follow me," he said and led her into an office

backstage. She picked up her bag, opened it, and rifled through the contents eagerly.

"Is everything there?" the man asked.

"Eh, yes—yes."

He requested that she sign a paper releasing the Hoaxters from any liability. Señora Mendez did so, then hurried back to where the girls were waiting for her.

"Is everything all right?" Bess asked her.

"Fortunately yes."

Nancy hoped this was true. She felt, however, that she should warn Señora Mendez. "There is a possibility the Hoaxters looked at your property and found something pals of theirs could use to either swindle or blackmail you. Please call your bank and request them to hold any check they suspect is a forgery. Also, don't let any fast-talking salesmen con you into dishonest schemes, either by telephone or in person."

The woman promised to do so. "Now you have me a bit frightened," she said. "Shall I call the police when something happens?"

"Yes," Nancy replied, "and if you need our help, we'll be glad to do whatever we can. We're amateur detectives."

"Where are you staying?" Señora Mendez asked.

"At the Fortunato," Nancy replied and wrote

their names on a piece of paper. She handed it to the woman. Señora Mendez, in turn, gave Nancy her address and telephone number.

"Have you any plans for tomorrow?" she asked.

Nancy said no, and the friendly Mexican immediately invited the girls to visit the Pyramid of the Sun with her. Intrigued by the name of the ancient monument, the young sleuths accepted eagerly. Señora Mendez promised to pick them up at ten the following morning. When she arrived, Nancy and her friends were waiting in the lobby.

On the way Bess complimented Señora Mendez on her expert handling of the car. The traffic was fast and appeared dangerous.

"You're brave," Bess said. "I wouldn't like to drive here."

"We'll soon be out of the city," the woman replied with a smile. "The roads will be less busy then."

"How far is the pyramid?" George asked.

"About twenty-five miles," Señora Mendez said. Then she told the girls some stories of ancient Mexico.

"There's one legend which I have always liked," she said. "Native Indians were standing on the shore of the ocean when they saw a huge fish approaching. A white man was seated on its back. Since the Indians had never seen a white man, they were sure he must be a god. When he landed, they knelt before him and he became their ruler for many years."

"Where did he come from?" Nancy asked.

"Apparently from Europe. The legend does not say at what point he got astride the fish, which was probably a friendly dolphin. No doubt he was a crewman from a shipwrecked vessel and was rescued by the dolphin."

"Lucky fellow," Nancy said with a chuckle.

Señora Mendez smiled. "When the man became old, he longed to go back to his own land. The last time the Indians saw him, he was climbing onto a dolphin's back to leave Mexico."

"What a charming story!" Bess remarked.

George laughed. "And a pretty preposterous one."

Nancy did not have time to comment because Señora Mendez immediately launched into another tale.

"No one is sure when the first Indians settled around Mexico City. Archeologists, who have been digging here for many years, believe it was at least four thousand years ago. One group after another came to fight the inhabitants. If the new arrivals won the battle, they immediately imposed their own political, religious, and ethical ideas on the captured people. Our present-day ruins are all that is left of the Aztec and earlier civilizations."

"Did the Aztecs build the Pyramid of the Sun?" Nancy asked.

"Not according to some scholars who say it was part of a Toltec tribe's city that was a thousand years old when the Aztec people came to power."

"The Aztecs were a highly intelligent and cultured people," George put in.

"That's true," Señora Mendez said. "And now look up ahead. There's the Pyramid of the Sun."

The enormous, broad-based structure rose in steps straight up into the blue sky with only a few fluffy clouds to soften its stark lines.

"What are those other buildings?" Bess asked.

"There's the smaller Pyramid of the Moon," Señora Mendez pointed out, "and in the distance are a number of pyramids, temples and burial spots, including the well-known Temple of Quetzalcoatl. All these were built on both sides of an ancient road about four miles long, known as the Highway of the Dead."

Bess shivered. "Not a very inviting name."

Señora Mendez smiled as she parked the car in a lot some distance from the pyramid. "I assure you there is nothing scary about this place," she added as they headed toward the imposing structure.

Señora Mendez told them that the pyramid had been erected in honor of the Sun God whom the Indians worshipped.

"It certainly is huge," George remarked.

"Yes, two hundred and sixteen feet high," their Mexican friend explained, "and seven hundred and fifty feet around the square base."

On the side facing them shallow stone steps led to the top. Several people were ascending.

"Do you feel like climbing?" Señora Mendez asked.

"Oh, yes," the girls chorused.

"What's at the top?" Bess wanted to know.

"Nothing now," was the reply. "But a thousand years ago it was very different. Prisoners of war were marched up the steps and slain at the top by priests."

"Ugh!" Bess murmured. "I'm not sure I want to go up after all."

Señora Mendez said that there was nothing left to remind anyone of that cruel custom. "But there's a magnificent view which you shouldn't miss."

Bess finally consented to go. She was the last in line and after a while the rest of the group had advanced far ahead of her.

Suddenly a middle-aged woman a few feet above Bess cried out, "Oh, I'm falling! I feel faint! Save me! Save me!"

No one was near her except Bess, who saw the woman teeter, then begin to tumble down the steps.

"I must catch her before she hurts herself!" Bess

thought frantically. But she knew that if she remained in front of the stranger, she herself would be knocked down by the impact.

A quick thought flashed through Bess's mind. She had once read that in climbing or descending mountains or monuments, the Indians always zigzagged their way. They would take a dozen steps to the right, then to the left. This not only kept them from falling but helped conserve their breath.

Bess turned and braced herself. She caught the woman around her shoulders. Both teetered for a few seconds, then Bess regained her footing and started down sideways, dragging the woman with her.

By this time several tourists had hurried to the scene. Two husky men came up to meet Bess and her burden. They lifted the unconscious figure over their shoulders and carried her to the ground.

Bess was relieved. Thinking what might have happened, she was also nervous and upset. With shaking knees she sat down, trying to recuperate.

The woman who had fainted soon revived. When she learned of Bess's help, she called out in English, "Thank you very much for saving me! You're so brave you should have a medal!"

Bess was embarrassed by the praise. Quickly she rose, waved to the woman and hurried up the steps.

Her friends, who were close to the top, had heard the shouting. When Bess joined them, Nancy said, "That was a wonderful rescue!"

George patted her cousin on the shoulder. "Just great!" she added.

"Oh, forget it, everybody," Bess murmured. "Did you find any skeletons here?"

"No," Nancy replied. "But let's walk around a little while. Then I think we should go back to the hotel. Señora Mendez has been very kind, but we've taken enough of her time."

Bess agreed. "I'm rather weary myself."

The group descended and had reached the last step, when Nancy grabbed George by one arm.

"Look over there!" she exclaimed, and pointed to a man who was rounding a corner of the pyramid. Isn't that Enzo Scorpio, the poison thief?"

"He sure is," George answered.

She turned and ran in his direction. Nancy was close on her heels, and Bess followed. Señora Mendez stood still, staring after the girls in amazement.

Just then the suspect saw them. Quick as a wink he turned back and disappeared behind the great pyramid!

# 8

## Startling News

The chase went on for some time. Nancy, Bess, and George took different routes to head off the fleeing suspect. They climbed up and down the steps of the Sun Pyramid, until the fugitive dashed away in a southerly direction. He ran toward the famous Temple of Quetzalcoatl. Even though Nancy concentrated hard on the chase, she could not help but admire the elaborate rows of carvings on the ancient structure depicting the fabled plumed serpent in whose honor the temple had been erected.

Suddenly Enzo Scorpio headed for the parking lot. Nancy had nearly caught up with the man when he jumped into a car, started the engine in a split second and roared away. His wheels churned

up a cloud of dust. Some of it hit Nancy full force as she came almost close enough to touch the vehicle's rear fender.

Coughing, she stopped short and bit her lips in frustration. Despite her anger, she managed to read the license number of the automobile. As soon as the dust had settled somewhat, she pulled a piece of paper out of her handbag and wrote the number down.

Bess caught up to her with George not far behind.

"What happened?" she asked.

"I almost had him, but he jumped into a car and took off!" Nancy replied.

"What terrible luck!" George exclaimed.

"Where's Señora Mendez?" Bess inquired.

The girls looked around and noticed the woman going toward her car. Quickly they followed.

As Nancy passed an athletic-looking young man, who was obviously from the United States, he said, "Want me to chase that guy with my car?"

"Thank you, no," Nancy replied.

The young man smirked. "If you're after a handsome fellow, how about me?"

The girls ignored his remarks and continued toward Señora Mendez. When they reached her, she asked why the girls had chased the stranger. Nancy explained and the woman was shocked.

"He stole a vial of dangerous poison?" she cried out. "He certainly should be put in prison for that!"

The girls agreed. Then Bess declared that she had had enough sightseeing and exercise for the day and would like to return to the Fortunato. Señora Mendez nodded and drove the girls to Mexico City.

When they reached their hotel room, Nancy at once phoned Lieutenant Tara.

"Before we left New York," she said, "a vial of poison was stolen from a friend of ours. We were told that the New York police suspect a man named Enzo Scorpio of the theft. We just saw him at the Pyramid of the Sun!"

"You know him?" Lieutenant Tara asked.

"Yes," Nancy replied and told the officer about their visit to Mr. Horner's medical laboratory. "We chased Enzo Scorpio, but he got away in a car," she added and gave the lieutenant the license number.

Tara thanked her and promised to track down the car. "I hope we can find out where Scorpio lives," he said.

Later in the afternoon he called back and told Nancy that the trail had led to a dead end. The car used by the poison thief had been rented but not by Enzo Scorpio. The man who had signed for the automobile had shown his license and given his address. When the police tried to contact him, they learned he had left town.

"We have no idea where he went or when he'll be back," the lieutenant told Nancy. "But if we manage to find out, we'll let you know."

Nancy was thoughtful for a moment, then said, "I think Scorpio will try to sell the vial to a collector. Do you know of any in Mexico City?"

"Hm," Lieutenant Tara said. "As a matter of fact, I do. He is a well-to-do man who has a large collection of ancient poison vials. His name is Fernando Pedroa. Ordinarily he would not be allowed to have them in his house, but we know he's trustworthy and gave him a special permit to keep the poisons. They are securely locked in a separate room."

Nancy said she and her friends would like to meet the man if possible. "Could you give us a letter of introduction?"

Lieutenant Tara chuckled. "I am sure that Señor Pedroa would love to see you and hear about the mystery. He's a very pleasant man. I will send a note of introduction to your hotel."

"Thank you," Nancy said.

A short time later a messenger brought the letter. "Let's call on the collector right away," Nancy proposed to Bess and George.

When they arrived at their destination in a taxi,

she asked the driver to wait until they found out if Señor Pedroa was at home.

Nancy rang the doorbell and a servant answered. He told her that Señor Pedroa was in the garden. She handed over the letter from Lieutenant Tara. While the servant went to deliver it, George paid the cabbie and dismissed him.

In a few minutes Señor Pedroa came to welcome the girls. He ushered them into his beautifully furnished living room. When the Mexican learned that Bess and George knew no Spanish, he spoke to them in fluent English.

Nancy quickly outlined their case about the poison, then asked if Enzo Scorpio had tried to sell him the ancient vial. The answer was no.

"We have seen this man in Mexico City," Nancy explained. "He worked for a medical laboratory in New York. Enzo Scorpio stole the vial from a friend of ours. The lab owner said the gold filigree poison container was made in the fifteenth century and is probably extremely valuable. The poison in it is still potent."

Señor Pedroa's eyes lighted up. "If it is a genuine piece it would be very valuable. I'd buy the vial if it were offered to me."

"We found it in a Florentine costume," Bess spoke up. "No one knows how long it was there."

Señor Pedroa smiled. "And you believe this

Enzo Scorpio stole the poison? What makes you so sure it was he?"

"The New York police told us. Enzo is a Mexican, so they suggested we look for him here."

George added, "When we went sightseeing at the Pyramid of the Sun this morning, we saw Scorpio. He noticed us and escaped in a car."

Señor Pedroa shook his head in amazement. "You girls are certainly wonderful detectives. I would like to help you solve your mystery. If I hear from Enzo Scorpio I'll contact you at once."

"And please notify the police." Nancy urged.

The man promised to do so, then asked if the girls would like to see his collection of antique poison containers.

"Oh, yes," they chorused.

He unlocked a heavy metal door. Behind it was a room lighted by fluorescent tubes. On the walls were bars so close together that no hand could reach through to the shelves behind them.

"I have to be sure that nothing will be stolen," Señor Pedroa explained. The glass-encased shelves were divided into compartments. In each stood a beautiful, handcrafted container.

"Many of them still have poison inside," the Mexican went on. "I try to trace the origin and find out what it is. But I'm not always successful. All these vials are old. They are genuine and valuable."

George pointed to a case filled with rings. "Are those the kind that hold poison?" she asked.

"You are correct," Señor Pedroa replied. "As you may know, poison rings date back to classical times. The great General Hannibal killed himself by drinking the fluid contained in the cap of such a ring."

Bess grimaced. "How awful!"

Señor Pedroa smiled. "You are right. It is not a subject we should dwell on. How about a cup of tea?"

"Thank you!" the girls accepted with alacrity.

He locked his collection room, then led the visitors onto a sunny patio, where the servant brought trays of luscious-looking petit fours and jam tarts. Bess had not thought about being hungry, but suddenly declared she was starved.

The servant poured tea for everyone and passed around the delicious cakes. By the time the girls stood up to leave, all of them were sure they would not need any dinner!

Nancy told Señor Pedroa, "We've had a delightful and informative visit. Thank you."

Their gracious host admitted he had enjoyed their company immensely and wished them luck in solving the mystery of the missing vial of poison.

When Nancy and her friends arrived at the Fortunato, they found a message for them at the desk.

Rosa Mendez had called and left her phone number.

"Please contact me at once," was written underneath the number.

The girls hurried to their room and Nancy put in the call. Señora Mendez recognized her voice and began to sob. She was barely able to speak and Nancy could hardly understand her.

"Please, Señora Mendez, say that again," she requested.

The woman cried out, "My granddaughter, Dolores, has been kidnapped!"

# 9

## Stage Attack

"Kidnapped? When? How?" Nancy asked Rosa Mendez, utterly shocked.

Between sobs the woman explained that her nine-year-old granddaughter had been on her way home from school. When she did not arrive for hours after the expected time, her parents called the police.

"My daughter," Señora Mendez went on, "also phoned Dolores's teacher, who was amazed that the child had disappeared. Dolores had stayed late after class to help straighten the classroom, then started for home. The teacher got in touch with other students and asked if they knew where Dolores had gone."

"Did she have any success?" Nancy asked.

"Yes. Two girls saw Dolores get into a car. They had assumed that the driver and the woman in the back seat were friends or relatives. The girls were dreadfully upset to hear that their playmate had been kidnapped."

"I'm so sorry," Nancy said. "I'll do all I can to help you find her. Have you any clues?"

"There are none," the Mexican woman replied. "Oh, why did the kidnappers have to pick out *my* family?"

Nancy said, "I have suspected the Hoaxters of dishonesty for some time. They ask people to come on stage and by sleight of hand remove their possessions. They probably look among the articles to find out who of the owners are wealthy, influential, or famous. That's why I tried to hold you back when you went on stage. In your case, the men might have learned that you have a sizable bank account and also a darling granddaughter whom you adore."

"Oh, yes, I do," Señora Mendez cried out and began to sob again.

Nancy tried to calm her by saying, "I'm sure that either you or your daughter and her husband will receive a ransom note. Or you may get a phone message directly from Dolores."

"I hope we do. Then at least we would know that she is all right."

81

"I agree," Nancy said. "Please call me the instant you hear from the abductors. Meanwhile," she added, "I suggest you keep your phone line free in case the kidnappers or even the police want to get in touch with you."

"You are so wise," Señora Mendez said. "I will not talk any longer. But I'm very upset."

"You have good reason to be," Nancy told her. "Please try to calm down. Think only good thoughts for your granddaughter's return."

After saying good-by, Nancy told Bess and George what had happened. The girls were thunderstruck and agreed that Nancy's hunch about the Hoaxters was no doubt correct.

"I also think," Nancy told them, "that there is more to it than I have guessed so far. If the Hoaxters are successful in drawing capacity crowds, why should they need to be mixed up with con men and kidnappers?"

George nodded. "And why was it necessary for them to run away from New York?"

Bess was not listening. Instead she said, "I feel sorry for poor little Dolores. Oh, I hope she's not being mistreated! The poor child! She must be so frightened."

Nancy proposed that they go at once to the theater where the Hoaxters were performing and try to find out if her hunch really was correct.

Just then their telephone rang. Señora Mendez was calling again. She was very excited.

"We've had news!" she said. "My daughter and her husband received a hand-delivered note. But the person who brought it hurried away before they could ask him any questions. This is what the note said:

"Your daughter will not be harmed, but she will be taken on a long journey."

"Is that all?" Nancy asked.

"Yes. And while we're relieved to know that Dolores is all right, we are extremely worried about this long journey. They might even take the child out of the country!"

Nancy conceded this was possible. The question was, why did the kidnapper plan to take their hostage away from Mexico City?

The young detective asked, "You're sure there was no demand for money?"

"Positive," Señora Mendez answered. "Well, Nancy, I won't talk any longer. But as soon as I have more information, I'll let you know."

The girls resumed their plan to attend the Hoaxters' performance. Nancy wanted to ask their leader point-blank why they kept people's possessions for at least half an hour.

She hailed a cab which let the girls off in front of the theater. No one was standing outside. Since it was an hour before show time, Nancy thought nothing of this. The front door was locked. George noticed a bell button and pushed it.

After a long wait, a maintenance man appeared. "What do you want?" he asked gruffly in Spanish.

Nancy told him that it was imperative the girls talk to the manager of the Hoaxters at once.

"He's not here. None of them are."

"When will they arrive?" Nancy asked in surprise.

"Maybe never."

"What do you mean?"

The man said the troupe had packed up suddenly and left. Nancy turned to Bess and George and quickly translated the information.

George said, "This is the second time they've skipped out of town!"

"And maybe they did it before that," Bess added.

Nancy addressed the maintenance man. "Is the manager of the theater in?"

The employee hesitated, then reluctantly opened the door. "I'll take you to his office," he said.

The maintenance man explained that the young ladies had come to talk with the manager, then went back to his work.

The gray-haired Mexican looked at them closely. "What's so important that you have to see me?" he asked.

Nancy noticed a sign on his desk with the name Señor Tomás on it. She explained that they had followed the Hoaxters from New York because certain people believed the troupe might not be honest.

"Do you know where they went?" she asked.

"No," Señor Tomás replied. "They left a note and enough money to cover the theater rental for the period they had reserved. I believe they departed last night."

"No one saw them go?" Nancy asked.

Señor Tomás explained that after the evening's performance which ended close to midnight, no one else had been in the building. Apparently a car or truck had been driven to the rear of the theater and loaded with the Hoaxters' props.

"When we arrived this morning, we discovered that all their possessions were gone," he added.

"Thank you very much," Nancy said. "Do you mind if we girls look around a bit to see if we can pick up a clue as to where the Hoaxters went?"

The manager glanced at them, puzzled. Finally he said, "Are you detectives?"

Nancy smiled. "Just amateurs. We're trying to help a friend."

Señor Tomás gave his permission and the group walked into the theater. No one was there. The girls went down a stairway to the dressing rooms. They noticed the maintenance man cleaning the floor.

He stared at them. "What are you doing here?" he demanded in Spanish.

Nancy replied, "We're just looking around."

The man became belligerent. "Looking around, eh? You're spying on me! Well, get out of here and fast!"

Although Bess and George could not understand him, they knew he was angry about something.

Bess said, "Nancy, we'd better go."

The cleaning man pointed to the door and motioned for the girls to leave. Fortunately Señor Tomás arrived just at that moment. When he heard about the altercation, he told his employee that the girls had his permission to survey the premises. They could stay as long as they wished. He added that the young detectives were trying to find clues to where the Hoaxters had gone.

"Do you know?" the manager asked him.

"No, I don't," the man replied. "And if I did, I wouldn't tell anyone. When a fellow wants to keep something secret, other folks have no right to pry."

"That's enough from you!" the manager reprimanded him. "And leave the girls alone!"

The cleaning man looked sullen and continued to mop the floor. Nancy thanked Señor Tomás, who left with a nod. Together, the girls went through the various dressing rooms but found nothing to indicate the whereabouts of the Hoaxters.

"This place is big!" George remarked. "Why don't we split up? That way we can cover more space."

"Good idea," Nancy agreed and the girls separated.

In a few minutes Nancy found herself on the stage. In the dim light it was difficult for her to spot anything the Hoaxters might have left. As she stood still, thinking about the mystery, something heavy suddenly crashed over her head. It almost knocked her to the floor!

Dizzily she struggled to extricate herself from the object and finally succeeded. Before her lay an oil painting that she had seen hanging on the wall during one of the Hoaxters's routines.

As she thought of it around her neck like a hoop, Nancy chuckled. Then her face became grim. "That painting didn't fall on me by accident!" she thought. "Someone deliberately jammed it down over my head!"

She looked in all directions but saw no one. "I'll bet it was that disgruntled cleaning man," she reasoned.

Just then a pretty Indian woman with a mop and bucket walked onto the stage. She stared at Nancy in amazement. Noticing her rumpled hair and disheveled blouse, she asked in Spanish what had happened.

Nancy explained and the Indian shook her head in sympathy. "That is very bad!" she declared. "I am glad you were not hurt."

The woman introduced herself as Sara. Then the girl detective asked her if she had seen anyone on stage a few moments before.

"Yes," Sara replied, "the maintenance man."

"I thought it was he," Nancy said.

She now questioned the woman about the Hoaxters's sudden departure.

Sara said she had not heard why the troupe had disappeared. "I did not like them," she added. "I think they were up to no good!"

"Have you any idea where they went?" Nancy asked.

Sara suddenly looked frightened. "I know, but they threatened to harm me if I told anyone!"

"Oh!" Nancy exclaimed. Here was a wonderful clue, the young sleuth thought, but how could she persuade Sara to tell her what it was?

# 10

## A Setback Reversed

The cleaning woman began to mop the floor. Nancy was afraid that she would not reveal where the Hoaxters had gone. While the young detective tried to figure out how to persuade Sara, she picked up a dust cloth and wiped off the stage furniture.

Sara looked at her and smiled. Nancy smiled back. "Sara, if the Hoaxters have left, how can they harm you?"

The woman hesitated, then replied, "You are right. I overheard the men say they were going to Los Angeles. They realized I was standing close enough to hear their conversation, and accused me of eavesdropping. But I had no such intention.

That was when they threatened to harm me if I told anyone."

"I'm glad you *did* tell me," Nancy said. "Los Angeles is a long way from here. I wouldn't worry if I were you."

Sara was relieved. She told Nancy that ever since seeing the men take wallets and handbags she had not trusted the performers. "I think they ran away because something happened," she said. "But I have no idea what it was."

Nancy wondered about the information. Suddenly she had an idea: No doubt one of the patrons complained to the police about having to give up his wallet until the end of the show. The police in turn must have asked the Hoaxters to come to headquarters and explain. Since they want nothing to do with the authorities, they left. The same thing probably happened in New York!

"Sara," she said to the woman, "the maintenance man wasn't very nice to us when we came in. Is he always so grumpy?"

Sara glanced up from the mop she was using.

"I do not like him. He does as little work as he can get away with and is forever looking for tips. The Hoaxters gave him big ones. I know because he used to brag about it."

"Did he receive large tips because he did special favors for the magicians?"

Sara shrugged. "I do not know, but it is possible. Or perhaps he found out some secret of theirs and they paid him to keep quiet."

Nancy changed the subject. "Did anyone not connected with the show ever come here to see the Hoaxters?"

"Oh, yes. Two fellows came twice. One was called Howie, the other Lefty. They arrived after the performance and talked to the Hoaxters in a dressing room with the door locked. No one else could hear what they were saying."

At this moment George and Bess arrived on stage. Nancy introduced them to Sara and said the woman had given her some good clues.

"Did you girls learn anything?" Nancy asked.

"Nothing," Bess replied.

George added, "At one point the cleaning man followed me though the theater, but I managed to avoid him. I didn't come across anything to help solve the mystery, however."

Sara had nothing else to contribute either, so the girls said good-by to her, walked off the stage and out the back door.

"Sara mentioned Howie and Lefty visiting the Hoaxters," Nancy told Bess and George excitedly. "I'm sure that was Howie Barker. I wonder who Lefty is."

"Maybe he's another con man," Bess offered.

While the three girls were waiting for a taxi in

front of the theater, Nancy brought her friends up to date on her conversation with Sara.

"Well, where do we go from here?" Bess asked.

"To Los Angeles!" Nancy replied promptly.

As soon as they reached the Fortunato Hotel, she called the airport to make reservations. As Nancy hung up, she frowned.

"No flights?" George asked.

"An air strike just started and may last for a month!" Nancy responded. "What'll we do now?"

"Drive," Bess suggested.

"Do you realize how far it is?" Nancy asked.

"Over twenty-five hundred miles!" George answered.

"Right. It'll take us five days if we drive ten hours a day!"

"That's better than staying here for a month," George declared.

"I suppose so," Nancy said unenthusiastically.

Bess sighed. "I'm not looking forward to that long haul either. But we can take turns driving and perhaps even make it in four days."

Nancy nodded. "Okay. Let's rent a car tomorrow."

The next day directly after breakfast their telephone rang. Señora Mendez was calling. She sounded hysterical.

"Oh, Nancy, come here at once. Please!" the woman sobbed.

"What happened?"

Señora Mendez said she could not tell her over the phone, but she had something very important to show the three sleuths.

"We'll take a taxi and be over as soon as possible," Nancy promised.

When the girls arrived at her residence, the Mexican woman showed them a letter that she said had been left on the front doorstep.

"My maid heard a knock and went to answer it. When she opened the door, no one was there but the letter lay on the mat. She brought it to me and I almost fainted. Please read it."

Nancy unfolded the note that was flat but originally had been folded like a fan. It was on a long, narrow sheet of paper and the words that ran from top to bottom were composed of letters or words cut from a newspaper. The message was:

Get
ready
to
deliver
$100,000
ransom
in
unmarked
bills
in
a
small
light-

94

weight
sack
in
hundred
dollar
denominations
to
assure
release
of
Dolores
8
hours
later
totally
unharmed
by
her
poor
needy
abductors.
X
directions
will
follow

"Have you called your daughter?" Nancy asked.

"Yes. She has heard nothing. I told her I would gladly pay the money, but she is afraid Dolores may not be returned even though the ransom is paid. That's why I'm so upset. I don't know what to do and I can't ask anybody to help me!"

"Why not?" Nancy countered. "We girls will continue to work on the mystery for you."

The woman pointed out there was another part to the note that they had not read yet.

"Turn it over," she directed.

The remainder of the message warned Señora Mendez that harm would come to Dolores and her family if anyone contacted police or detectives.

The Mexican woman walked up and down the living room in great agitation. "So you see," she said, "I'll have to ask you girls to forget the case!"

Nancy, Bess, and George were stunned. They appreciated the grandmother's concern about the safety of her family, but the young sleuths did not want to give up trying to find the child.

Nancy went to the distraught woman and put an arm around her shoulders. "We are not part of the police and we are not professional detectives," she said soothingly. "We are only amateurs and the note does not include us. Please let us continue to work on your case."

Señora Mendez hugged Nancy and kissed her, then consented to let the girls proceed in their hunt.

"But what can you possibly do?" she asked. "You have no idea where the kidnappers have taken my Dolores!"

"We suspect," Nancy replied, "that the Hoaxters are involved in this, as I told you before." She paused.

"Yes, yes, go on," the woman urged.

"We found out," Nancy continued, "that they have gone to Los Angeles. Possibly they took Dolores with them. The whole troupe left here abruptly without giving the theater manager any advance notice."

"Oh, if you could only find Dolores!" Señora Mendez said, gazing at the three girls in admiration.

Nancy examined the ransom note more carefully, reading the words over and over. "I believe there's a code message hidden in the wording."

"It's hidden all right," Bess commented.

"A message for whom?" George asked.

Nancy replied, "My guess would be that it was intended for someone connected with the kidnappers."

"But why would it be folded again and again before being sent to Señora Mendez?" Bess questioned.

Nancy was thoughtful. "Perhaps this folded note was not meant for her. It could have been delivered to Señora Mendez by mistake. Suppose there were two identical notes," Nancy went on. "One was folded, the other not even creased. The plain one may have been the ransom note for Señora Mendez, the folded one a copy for a confederate."

"I still don't get it," Bess admitted.

"The clue to a hidden message for the confederate must be in the folds!" Nancy declared.

"But there's a fold under every word," Bess said.

"That's the strangest kind of code I ever heard of."

"Maybe the fan is the identification of the group." Nancy said.

"You know," George spoke up, "this reminds me of a game we used to play as children. A sheet of paper and a pencil were passed around a group. Each player would write one line, then fold the paper over and give it to the next person. When all the players had written on it, someone would open it and read the story. Usually it was a silly one about somebody in the group. Once the paper said I was a mad elephant who liked to dance!"

Nancy was not paying strict attention. She was already working to decipher the ransom note. First she read every second fold, next every third, then the fourth.

Suddenly she cried out, "I have it! The code is in every fifth word!"

"Well, Sherlock Holmes, what does it say?" Bess urged.

Nancy smiled and replied, "It says, '$100,000 in sack to 8 by X.'"

"Hm," said Bess. "To me that makes no sense at all. If that's a code, how are you ever going to break it?"

"Yes, how?" George challenged her.

Nancy replied, "I don't know, but I'm not giving up. We must solve this! It's too good a clue not to follow!"

# 11

## An Odd Invention

"I think the 8 and the X are the solution to the puzzle," Nancy said. "The 8 could stand for the eighth letter of the alphabet, namely H for Howie. But 'by X'?"

"The twenty-fourth letter of the alphabet," George said. "Or perhaps it signifies the twenty-fourth day of the month."

"Or it could mean a signature," Bess volunteered. "People who cannot write sign their name by making an X."

George sighed. "It's hard to be a detective. You have to be clairvoyant!"

Nancy laughed. "There are more possibilities."

"Oh, no!" Bess shook her head in desperation.

"Perhaps the message was not meant for a con-

federate of the kidnappers at all, but for us!"
Nancy suggested.

"I don't understand."

"Maybe the crooks want to lure us to a certain
spot on a certain day where they can set up a trap!"

"Oh, don't say such a thing," Bess begged. "You
make chills go up and down my spine."

"Calm down, my dear cousin," George said with
a chuckle. "I'm sure if our enemies want to trap us
they would have left more specific directions!"

Nancy asked Señora Mendez if any of the girls'
guesses gave her a clue to the solution of the
puzzle.

The woman shook her head. "Nothing occurs to
me," she replied. "Do you think it could refer to
something in Los Angeles?"

"We'll try to find out when we get there," Nancy
replied.

After making an exact copy of the ransom note,
the girls said good-by to their Mexican friend and
left. On the way back to the hotel they stopped at a
car rental agency. Nancy told the owner where the
girls wanted to go.

He smiled and said, "My partner flew to New
York last week and now has to go to Los Angeles
for a month or so. He wants someone to bring his
car to him. We'll be glad to give it to you as a rental
and you can leave it in Los Angeles. Usually we

require our cars to be returned to this country."

"Great!" Nancy said. "I suppose we came just at the right time."

The manager nodded. "The car will be ready for you to pick up by seven o'clock tomorrow morning."

The girls were happy with the arrangement and left the agency.

"We'll have some free time this afternoon," Bess said. "Why don't we go back to Señora Clara's dress shop and see if we can find another Mexican outfit?"

George smiled. "I haven't any money to spend, but I wouldn't mind looking."

When the girls arrived at Señora Clara's, no customers were in the shop. The friendly woman greeted them with a smile. "Hello again. Look around all you wish," she said. "I'll be busy for a while because a man is coming to offer me some wonderful new stock."

"What kind of stock?" Nancy asked, intrigued at once.

"In a company that has developed a fabulous fabric," Señora Clara explained. "It sounded very interesting."

To Nancy it sounded like a scheme the con men would invent, and she was suspicious at once. "Did you by any chance see a performance of the Hoaxters when they were in town?" she asked the dress shop owner.

"Yes, indeed," Señora Clara replied. "Weren't they fantastic?"

"They were," Nancy admitted. "Did you go up on stage?"

"Yes."

"I must tell you something we found out regarding the group that might concern you." Nancy explained the girls' suspicions and the various things that had happened to people who had attended the show.

Señora Clara was alarmed. "You mean the man who is coming here might try to swindle me?"

"It's quite possible," Nancy replied.

"But what shall I do? I have already made the appointment."

"Don't buy anything," George advised.

Señora Clara agreed. "Perhaps you would like to stay with me and see if you recognize the caller."

"We'd be glad to," Nancy said. "If he's Howie Barker, he would recognize us, so may we hide somewhere? Perhaps in a spot where we can get a good look at him?"

"Of course. One of the dressing rooms has a perfect view of my desk," Señora Clara declared. "And since I have no private office, this is where I'll sit when I talk to the man."

"Good idea," Nancy said and the girls crowded into the small cubicle. Its louvered door had slats through which the young detectives could look.

"This will be perfect," Nancy said.

Señora Clara smiled. "Just don't sneeze!"

Bess giggled. "We'll do our best not to."

A few minutes later two men entered the shop. They were well-dressed, good-looking, and very polite. When the taller one came closer and addressed Señora Clara, the girls stiffened. He was Barker, the man who had tried to swindle Bess!

"My name is Barker," he said. "I spoke to you on the telephone a little while ago. This is my colleague, Mr. Cadwell. We would like to tell you about a new firm that has developed a most fantastic fabric."

"Please be seated," Señora Clara said and pointed to two chairs next to her desk.

Mr. Cadwell pulled a brochure out of his briefcase and handed it to Señora Clara. It showed a little girl wearing the same attire in different settings. One picture depicted spring, with the child sitting in a field of crocuses; the next one summer, where she was perched at the side of a pool. In the third picture the girl was climbing a tree with bright yellow and reddish leaves, and the fourth showed her seated on a sled surrounded by snow.

"You see," Mr. Cadwell said, "this material can be worn at any time of year. It has a natural, built-in thermostat which adjusts itself to the wearer's body temperature. It works for everyone in all climates!"

"That's amazing!" Señora Clara said. "You mean this fabric can be worn comfortably 365 days a year in all climates?"

"That is correct."

"Do you have a sample with you?"

"Certainly."

The man produced several pieces of cloth from his briefcase. They were of different colors and textures, but each felt like a lightweight wool.

Señora Clara examined the samples but said nothing.

"This fabulous new invention," Mr. Cadwell went on, "is called Silk-O-Sheen. It is not mass-produced yet, but the inventor is setting up his first plant. We offer stock in this venture to people in the clothing business for a mere ten dollars a share. Now, how much can I sign you up for, Señora Clara?"

Nancy, who had observed the scene closely from the girls' hiding place, bit her lips. Would Señora Clara fall for the swindle?

But the businesswoman had a ready answer. "I'd like to think about it first," she said. "Besides, I have to consult my accountant to see if I have any extra cash to invest."

"Surely you have money in your cash register right now?" Mr. Barker urged. "You can give us a down payment of 20 percent and pay for the rest later."

"I never make hasty decisions," Señora Clara said coolly. "If you will leave me your card, I'll be glad to let you know in a day or two."

The men, who had been extremely affable until now, stopped smiling. Cadwell put the samples and the brochure back into his briefcase and snapped it shut angrily.

The visitors got up and bowed curtly. "You are making a big mistake!" Mr. Cadwell said. "And I'm telling you . . ."

Just then his companion glanced at a nearby chair. On it lay a small cloth wallet with the name Bess embroidered on it. "Who else is here?" he asked.

Señora Clara did not answer but she got up to retrieve the wallet. Bess Marvin's heart began to pound. It was hers!

Barker hurried to the chair and picked up the wallet. Señora Clara plunged toward him, crying out, "Leave that alone! Give it to me!"

Quick as a flash Howie Barker opened the wallet and read Bess's full name on her driver's license. The next second the store owner grabbed the wallet, while the man dashed to the louvered door and yanked it open.

"So!" he cried out angrily. "You girls deliberately spied on us! You'll be sorry for this!"

With that, he and Mr. Cadwell sped furiously out of the shop.

# 12

## Smugglers

George and Nancy ran after the men but soon stopped. Barker and Cadwell had jumped into a chauffered car and were out of sight in the heavy traffic a few seconds later.

"I couldn't see the license plate," Nancy said in disappointment.

As she and George returned to the shop, Bess asked worriedly, "What did Barker mean by that threat?"

"I don't know," Nancy replied, "but he'll think up something to harass us."

Señora Clara looked at the girls, puzzled. Then she said, "You'd better watch your step. I think those men could be very mean, even dangerous!"

"I think so, too," Bess said, sighing. Then she

added, "Now that we've averted a disaster, I'd like to look at dresses."

Nancy laughed. "Go ahead. "I'll phone the police, meanwhile, and tell them what happened."

"Please do," Señora Clara said. "You can sit at my desk. And you know, Cadwell did not leave me a business card. That makes it even more obvious to me that they are swindlers."

Nancy reported the incident to the authorities while Bess bought a lovely summer dress. Then they said good-by to Señora Clara, who wished them luck.

Early the next morning Nancy went to the car rental garage to pick up the automobile for the girls' trip. As she entered the large parking area, she glimpsed a man hurrying out a side door.

"He looked like Howie Barker!" she thought and started to run after him.

Suddenly she stopped short, telling herself it was a good thing the man had not seen her. Otherwise he would guess that the girls were leaving Mexico City!

"If I caught him, I'd have no evidence anyway," she decided and went to her rented automobile.

When Nancy arrived at the hotel, the girls packed their belongings in the trunk of the car, then rode off. Because of their early start, they had not had breakfast. An hour later Bess declared that she could not go much longer without food.

"We're far away from the city already," she said. "I wonder where we could find something to eat."

George asked, "Would you like some Mexican food?"

Bess confessed that at this point she was starved and would eat any kind of food.

"How about an enchilada sundae?" George teased.

"With hot fudge and whipped cream? Yick!" Bess frowned.

George winked at Nancy. "I saw a sign with an arrow back at the last side road. I couldn't read it, but the sign had pictures of tortillas and enchiladas on it."

Nancy turned the car around immediately, then took the side road. About a mile ahead they came to an Indian settlement. Women were seated on the ground cooking over low stone fireplaces. When the girls stopped, the natives looked up and smiled. Several children ran to the Americans, followed by barking dogs. Nancy and her friends jumped out of the car and approached the women.

Bess asked, "Do you serve breakfast?"

The woman closest to her glanced at the others in her group. They all shrugged.

George said, "I guess they don't speak English."

Nancy tried the same question in Spanish, but the only word the women seemed to understand was *comer,* which meant "to eat." They bobbed their heads.

One of the women pointed to the food being prepared. There were different varieties of tortillas and enchiladas, eggs scrambled with hot peppers, strong cocoa, ripe pineapples, and small bananas.

"Why do they have to put hot peppers with the eggs?" Bess complained.

Nancy replied, "In Mexico peppers are used as a health food. One time, when there was a great polio epidemic all over the United States, doctors found that there was not a single case of the disease in Mexico. Upon inquiry they learned that this was due to the daily use of peppers in the native diet."

Bess said she would like to fix her own scrambled eggs. "Nancy, ask the lady if I may," she urged.

Although Nancy felt sure the women would not understand, she complied with Bess's request.

The Indians held a conference, then suddenly a young, pretty girl chattered something excitedly. She raced off, but soon returned holding a live hen that squawked and tried to wiggle out of the girl's arms. She held onto it tightly and talked in her Indian dialect. To the amazement of the Americans, the hen laid an egg in the girl's palm!

Nancy and her friends laughed. Apparently the

Indians had thought that Bess wanted a newly laid egg!

The girl handed it to Bess, who picked up an empty pan. She took some cooking fat from a crock and melted it. Then she broke the egg on the edge of the pan and quickly scrambled it with a wooden spoon. The natives smiled and shrugged.

Nancy and George decided to brave the already prepared scrambled eggs seasoned with hot peppers. Unlike Nancy, who laid the peppers aside, George bit into one. Her eyes bulged as the spicy vegetable stung her mouth. She swallowed it quickly and gulped down a piece of cooling pineapple.

"When it comes to food," Bess smirked, "I guess I am the only sensible one—besides Nancy, of course!"

George grimaced, then broke into a mischievous smile. "I guess I deserve that for teasing you so much about your forty-inch waist!"

"My waist isn't forty inches!" Bess declared, causing George to giggle.

"You two!" Nancy remarked, shaking her head.

After paying for the meal, the girls drove off. They joked for several miles.

George continued to tease Bess. "Alongside those really stout Indian women you looked pretty good."

Nancy remarked that the younger ones were very

attractive. "I guess the older people have wrinkled skin and squinting eyes from the harsh sunlight."

The girls took turns driving and went as far as they could each day. They stopped at motels only when they were too tired to go on. It was an exhausting and uneventful trip. Bess regretted many times that she had suggested they take a car instead of waiting for the air strike to end.

After lunch on the fourth day the young travelers reached the border. Here they were stopped by a customs official in a snappy-looking uniform.

"We have nothing to declare," Nancy told him.

He requested to see driver's license and looked at it closely. "Nancy Drew!" he asked. "You mean you are not going to declare certain property you are concealing."

"I don't know what you're talking about."

"I'll tell you. Hidden in your car is a valuable jade figurine that you stole from a museum in Mexico City!"

"What!" all three girls exclaimed, stunned.

"You must have us confused with someone else," Nancy declared. "We are not thieves and you will find nothing in this car except our personal belongings."

The official paid no attention to her remark. Instead, he asked for the key and opened the trunk. He pushed aside the girls' baggage and looked in back of the spare tire. Presently he pulled out a box that the young detectives had never seen before. Inside lay an exquisite piece of jade carved in the form of a boat with a woman in it surrounded by water lilies.

"How beautiful!" Bess cried out. "Officer, we never saw this before."

The man stared at her disdainfully. "You are all good actresses, but you have been caught. You are smugglers!"

Nancy firmly denied the charge. Disturbing thoughts raced through her mind. What would happen to her? Would she receive a heavy fine? Even be sent to jail if she could not pay?

She looked at the man. "Where did you get the tip that we were carrying this jade piece?"

The officer refused to answer.

Bess was frightened. She stared into the distance and saw a handsome young man who was also apparently a customs officer. While Nancy continued to argue with the official, Bess smiled coquettishly.

He smiled back at the pretty girl. "Is there anything I can do for you? You're much too cute to be in trouble."

Bess blurted out her story and even let her eyes become moist. This was too much for the young man. He took her by the arm and led the tearful girl back to the group. Then he addressed the official who had searched the car.

"Why don't we check with the police in Mexico City, Mr. Rivera? This young lady tells me Lieutenant Tara knows them and can confirm that they are amateur detectives working on a case. After all, the tip could have come from one of their enemies."

The older man bobbed his head. "You watch the girls while I go inside and call. But don't let them get away until I come back!"

He went into his office, and Bess thanked the young officer for his help. Soon Mr. Rivera returned. For the first time he smiled.

"All right, young ladies, I believe we can let you continue your journey. Lieutenant Tara told us he would vouch for you personally. And I will see to it that the jade piece is returned to the museum."

"Thank you," Bess said with a sigh of relief. "I could see all of us in jail for the next twenty years!"

After the girls had driven a distance into the United States, Nancy said to Bess, "Thanks for your help. That was clever of you to play on that handsome guy's sympathy."

George laughed. "It's a good thing your friend Dave Evans wasn't there. He'd have been green with jealousy!"

As dusk was settling, the girls reached Los Angeles. Since they had made no reservations, Nancy stopped at the first hotel they came to. George went inside to inquire about a room. When she returned to the car, her face had a worried look.

"What's the matter?" Bess asked.

"There's a big convention in town. Hundreds of detectives from all over the United States are meeting here, and no hotel or motel has any rooms left."

"What are we going to do?" Bess asked.

No one spoke for a few minutes, then suddenly George remembered something. "Former neighbors of ours moved out here last year," she announced. "They invited my family and friends to visit them any time. Suppose I phone them."

"Wonderful!" Bess said. "Do it right now."

George went into the hotel again and looked up her former neighbors' name in the phone book. Mrs. Vetter was delighted to hear from her.

"Where are you?" she asked.

When she was told about the girls' predicament, she said, "This is great! All of you come right over. We'd love to have you stay as long as you wish."

"Oh, thanks so much," George said. "You're a lifesaver."

When she walked out of the phone booth, her eyes were twinkling. Nancy and Bess, who had followed her into the lobby, were eager to hear what she had learned.

"Everything is okay," George reported. "The Vetters would love to have us visit."

Elated, the trio went outside again. They headed for their car which was parked a short distance from the hotel. It was not in sight!

Nancy was puzzled. "I'm sure we left it right here!"

The girls walked farther down the street. By the time they reached the next intersection, they knew that their car had been stolen!

"Oh, no!" Bess wailed. "Do you realize all our luggage is gone, too?"

# 13

## The Invisible Hand

George was angry. she stomped her foot on the sidewalk and exclaimed, "Can you imagine our car being stolen right in front of a hotel full of detectives?"

Bess was more upset over the loss of their baggage. "What are we going to wear?" she asked. "I don't have enough money with me to buy a new wardrobe."

Nancy tried not to show her agitation. "Why don't we do some sleuthing and see if we can find a clue to the thief?" she suggested.

The girls walked back to the spot where they had parked the automobile. A light truck stood in its place now, but Nancy noted a large, rumpled piece of paper underneath. She pulled it out.

"What's that?" George asked, curious.

Nancy spread it out. "A poster advertising the Hoaxters!" she exclaimed.

The cousins leaned forward to read it. The poster gave the name of the theater and the performance schedule.

"We're in luck!" Nancy said. "I have a hunch that one of the Hoaxters took our car. Let's go over to the theater immediately and find out!"

"But how did they know we were in Los Angeles?" Bess asked. "And what car we were driving?"

"They knew about the car because they planted the jade figurine in it," Nancy declared. "I thought I saw Howie Barker leaving the garage when I picked the car up. But I can't see how they could have possibly followed us all the way here."

"Perhaps they had one of their partners waiting at the border," George suggested. "When he realized that we were not being detained, he followed us."

"You're probably right," Nancy admitted. "When we arrived and went into the hotel, he took our car!"

Soon the girls reached the theater. A man stood at the front door. He was made up, with a gray wig, mustache, and beard. The girls did not recognize him.

Nancy decided not to speak to him. Instead, she led the way through an alley that opened into a fenced-in parking lot. It was bordered by the street behind the theater and was almost filled to capacity with cars belonging to patrons of the evening performance.

"Do you think ours might be here?" Bess asked tensely.

"I hope so," Nancy replied. "Let's separate and check them all."

Each girl took a section of the parking lot and walked up and down the rows. Suddenly Nancy spotted their rented car parked near the fence! She hurried up to it, took the keys from her handbag, and opened the trunk. To her relief, the girls' baggage was still there!

As she slammed the trunk lid shut again, Bess and George joined her. From a distance they had seen her stop and open the luggage compartment.

"Is everything safe?" Bess asked worriedly.

Nancy smiled at her friend. "All your clothes are intact. And now we'd better get out of here as quickly as possible."

The girls piled into the car. It took some maneuvering on Nancy's part to get away from the fence. When she finally drove through the gate into the street behind the theater, the gray-bearded man they had noticed earlier ran toward them.

He yelled at the top of his lungs, "Stop thief! Stop thief!"

George leaned out the window. "We didn't steal this car!" she shouted. But they were already too far away for the man to hear her.

Fortunately, there was little traffic on the back street and Nancy proceeded quickly. After a few blocks she noticed a policeman and stopped. She told him what had happened.

The officer promised to inform headquarters about the incident. "You will be required to come in and sign a report," he said. "Where are you staying?"

"At the Vetters' on Dale Drive," Nancy said. "Can you tell us how to get there?"

"Sure."

The policeman gave her directions, and twenty minutes later the girls pulled into the Vetters' driveway. A gray-haired couple came out to greet them.

"George, how are you!" Mrs. Vetter exclaimed, hugging her former neighbor. "And I remember your cousin Bess. She was at your house several times when I stopped by to see your mother."

George introduced Nancy, who was warmly welcomed by the friendly couple.

"We've heard so much about your mystery solving," Mr. Vetter said, "that I'm delighted to meet you at last. Now, if you girls will let me have the car key, I'll take your luggage inside."

Mrs. Vetter showed the visitors to an attractive guest room and soon they were unpacking their clothes.

"I think we should call home and tell everybody where we are," Bess said.

George yawned. "Do you realize what time it is? Eleven o'clock here. That means it's two in the morning in River Heights. We'll have to wait until tomorrow."

Mrs. Vetter had prepared a midnight snack. When the girls had finished unpacking they all sat around the dining room table to eat ham salad sandwiches and dainty chicken sandwiches. For dessert they had hot chocolate and tarts filled with plum jam.

"Oh, this is good," Bess declared. "We were so eager to get here that we skipped dinner."

George nodded. "I wasn't even hungry until I saw the food. And now I'd like to go to bed. I'm exhausted."

"Go right ahead," Mrs. Vetter said. "You can tell us all the news tomorrow."

Even though the girls were extremely tired, they awoke early the next morning. When they came downstairs, all of them realized that their hosts were not up yet.

"This is a good time to call home," Nancy declared. "I'll start with my father."

Mr. Drew had not left for his office, and she told him what had happened since she had last spoken to him. She also gave him the Vetters' address and phone number.

"And what news do you have?" she asked. "Is everything all right at home?"

"Fine," Mr. Drew said. "I've heard from Señor Pedroa in Mexico City. He said the police tracked down Enzo Scorpio, the poison thief, but the man disappeared before they could arrest him."

"That's too bad," Nancy said.

"Yes. And now Hannah would like to say hello to you," her father added and handed the phone to the housekeeper.

Hannah Gruen told Nancy she had received a call from the girls' friends, Ned, Burt, and Dave. "They want to come to the West Coast and join you," she reported.

"Wonderful!" Nancy exclaimed. "Hold the line while I speak to Bess and George."

She quickly discussed the request with her friends, and both were eager to see the boys. Just then Mrs. Vetter walked into the room. George asked her if she would mind having three more guests, and the woman smiled.

"Of course not! The more the merrier!"

"Thank you so much," Nancy said, then relayed the invitation to Hannah.

Later in the morning, the young detective called Señora Mendez in Mexico City. "What is the latest word on the kidnapping?" she asked.

"It is not good," the woman answered, her voice trembling. "I received another ransom note, telling me to put the money into a sack and deposit it in a certain trash container attached to a big eucalyptus tree outside of town."

"And you followed the instructions?" Nancy asked.

"Yes, I did. The kidnappers warned me not to tell the police, but I asked that two of their detectives watch the place secretly, and grab whoever came to take the ransom money."

"Were they successful?" Nancy asked eagerly.

"No. But the money is gone!"

"You mean the ransom disappeared but the police failed to catch the man?"

"Exactly. It seemed as if an invisible hand reached into the trash can and removed the sack. There was no trace of anyone coming or going."

Nancy was amazed to hear this. "Was the tree tall," she asked, "or a low one with lots of branches and leaves?"

"It was not too tall and spread out a good bit," Mrs. Mendez replied. "It was bushy and full. Why do you ask?"

"I think I know what happened," Nancy said. "The thief might have hidden in the treetop before the police detectives took up their positions. When it was dark, he shinnied down, took the sack, and retreated into the branches again until the following day. After he saw the police check the trash can and drive away, he probably felt it was safe to come down."

"Oh, Nancy, I'm sure you're right."

"Have you heard anything about Dolores?" the young detective asked.

Señora Mendez began to cry. "No, we have not. There was to be a phone call after the money had been picked up to tell us where we could find Dolores. But neither I nor my daughter and her husband have been contacted. We're frantic with worry!"

"That's dreadful and very unfair," Nancy remarked. "As you know, Señora Mendez, I believe that Dolores was taken to Los Angeles. I will hunt for her here. Please don't worry too much. Hold hopeful thoughts."

"I'll try," the woman replied, her voice still shaky. She begged the young sleuth to start work immediately. "And keep me informed about any clues you pick up. I will pray that you succeed."

When Bess, George, and the Vetters heard the report, they were aghast. All of them agreed that the kidnapper was a totally heartless person.

Later in the morning, Nancy was summoned to

police headquarters to make a formal charge against the thief who had stolen her rented car. When she returned to the Vetters, after dropping off the car at the designated address, George said, "Are they checking out the man who raced into the parking lot, yelling 'Stop thief!'?"

"Yes, they are," Nancy replied. "But even though I described him as best I could, he was so made up that it will be hard to identify him. Too bad we didn't recognize him by his voice."

Bess spoke up. "Well, I'm glad we didn't. I don't want to have anything to do with any kind of thief . . . carnapper, childnapper or dognapper, you name it!"

Nancy and George laughed. The subject was dropped for the time being, because the Vetters had invited some friends to their house to meet the girls. The party was scheduled for four o'clock and no one left until after nine. By then, the young sleuths had been so distracted by the conversation that they had almost forgotten why they had come to Los Angeles.

"But first thing tomorrow morning," Nancy said, "we must do some detective work."

That night everyone went to bed early. They had been asleep several hours, when suddenly all were awakened by the smoke alarm. It was beeping at a tremendous rate!

The girls jumped out of bed, put on bathrobes and slippers, then dashed into the hall. Their hosts had already hurried downstairs, and the young detectives followed. The house was full of smoke, so they rushed outdoors.

"Where's the fire?" Bess asked. "I don't see any flames."

"In the laundry room in the wing," Mr. Vetter answered.

He went to call the fire department, then picked up the garden hose. He played it through the windows of the laundry room, trying to extinguish the flames.

"My husband thinks someone set the fire deliberately," Mrs. Vetter declared.

The girls looked at her, shocked. Was the perpetrator one of their enemies?

# 14

## More Tricks

It was impossible for the Vetters and their guests to go into the laundry room. The smoke was too thick and acrid. Firemen soon arrived and quickly extinguished the blaze. Luckily not much damage had been done to the washer and dryer, but the walls were covered with soot and the floor was full of foamy water.

"This place is a mess," George remarked. "Mr. and Mrs. Vetter, I'm terribly sorry. There is a good chance that this fire was set by enemies of Nancy, Bess, and me."

"What do you mean?" one of the firemen asked, amazed.

George looked toward Nancy, as if requesting

her to carry on. The young sleuth nodded and gave the firemen a brief sketch of the case on which they were working.

"Hm," one of them said. "It does look as if you have a point, miss. Men, let's see what we can find."

After looking around carefully, they came upon a scorched can of inflammable fluid that had been hidden behind a hamper.

"Here's what was used to set the blaze," a fireman, who said his name was Scotty, told the Vetters and their guests. "I'll report all you've told me to the chief. Would you care to give me the names of the people you suspect?"

Mrs. Vetter interrupted. "Oh, Nancy, don't do that! You may be harmed if those wicked men find out you've reported them."

Nancy conceded that the woman had a point. Furthermore, she did not have a single bit of evidence to prove her accusation.

She said to Scotty, "I suppose I'd better not reveal any more at this time. I have no proof, only suspicions."

After the men had left, Mr. Vetter said he thought all of them should go back to bed. "We'll talk more about it in the morning."

As he closed the outside door to the laundry room, he asked his wife if she had left the door unlocked on purpose.

Mrs. Vetter shook her head. "I'm always very careful to lock it."

"Then whoever set the fire must have had a master key," her husband remarked. "There is no evidence here that the lock was forced."

Nobody slept very soundly for the rest of the night. Everyone wondered if the smoke alarm would go off again, or if something else might happen to the house. By morning Nancy said she was convinced that the girls' enemies had somehow tracked them down. But how?

"In any case," she said to Bess and George, "I think we should leave. It's not fair of us to put the Vetters through any more frightening experiences."

"I agree," Bess added.

George said, "Let me talk to them. After all, they're doing a good deed by giving us a place to stay while we're trying to find the con men and their associates."

Before Nancy or Bess could comment, George had hurried out of the room. To their surprise she returned in a few minutes.

"The Vetters won't hear of our leaving," she reported. "Both of them said they are enjoying this mystery, and besides," George chuckled, "they're looking forward to the boys' visit."

"Then that settles it," Bess said, giggling.

When the young detectives arrived at the breakfast table, Nancy thanked their hosts for such a generous attitude. "You're really good sports," she said. "And I think the fire proves we girls are on the right track of little Dolores's kidnappers."

Bess added, "We must be getting so close to them that they're trying to drive us out of Los Angeles."

"Well, they're not going to succeed!" George announced vehemently.

"I'd like to phone Dad," Nancy put in. "Maybe he's had news about the Maine hotel and the company that supposedly produces the Silk-O-Sheen fabric."

Mr. Drew reported that he had not been able to unearth anything. "The firms are probably fictitious, and any literature about them is phony, too," he declared. "But I need more time to prove it."

Nancy brought him up to date on what had happened since she had last talked to him. "It seems to me you're in great danger, Nancy," he said in concern. "Perhaps you had better come home."

"Oh, Dad, you don't mean that!" Nancy protested. "Besides, we'll get help soon. Ned, Burt, and Dave are coming out here."

"I know. Mrs. Marvin told me. Dave phoned her to get your address."

"What!" Nancy exclaimed. "When?"

"Yesterday morning."

"But I gave the boys our address myself. Dave didn't have to call Mrs. Marvin—and you know, I'm beginning to wonder if he did!"

"You mean it was an impostor who called?" Mr. Drew asked.

"Yes. Maybe the same man who started the fire in the Vetters' laundry room last night."

"But how would he know about Dave?"

"When the Hoaxters took Bess's handbag during the performance in New York, they probably found her picture of Dave with his name and address on it."

"Why don't you phone Dave and find out if he spoke to Mrs. Marvin?" Mr. Drew suggested.

"I'll do that right now. And thanks for the info, Dad."

Nancy hung up and dialed Dave's number. He answered promptly. When Nancy asked him if he had inquired about their address, he was amazed.

"Of course I didn't," he said. "Why should I? I already knew where you're staying."

"That's what I figured," Nancy replied. "But someone called Mrs. Marvin and soon afterwards a fire was set in the Vetters' laundry room."

Dave gasped. "I think we boys had better get to Los Angeles in a hurry. You need our protection!"

Nancy chuckled. "You may be right."

When the rest of the group heard about her conversation with Dave, they were convinced that the call to Mrs. Marvin had, indeed, been a ploy of the arsonist.

Nancy then got in touch with Señora Mendez. The woman told her that a third ransom note had been mailed to her from Mexico City.

"It told me to leave more money on a bench at an intersection near my home and promised Dolores would be set free after the ransom was paid."

"Did you comply with the request?"

"Yes. This time I hired a private detective, who carried a walkie-talkie so he could communicate with me. He dropped the package at the designated spot and walked away. He hid and kept watch from a distance."

"What happened?" Nancy asked eagerly.

"Nothing," Señora Mendez replied sadly. "No one picked up the money, and Dolores was not brought home. Oh, Nancy, what am I going to do?"

The girl took a deep breath. "Don't lose faith," she said. "I have a strong hunch that everything will turn out all right. Perhaps the kidnappers suspected that you had hired a detective and for that reason did not go through with the exchange. But I'm sure Dolores is fine."

"I hope you're right," Señora Mendez replied.

"I'm trying to keep calm, but my poor daughter is ill with worry."

Then the Mexican woman changed the subject. "I have a message for you, Nancy. I had a phone call from Señor Pedroa. He is the one you went to see about his collection of poisons, isn't he?"

"That's right."

"He said he couldn't reach your dad, so he left a message with me. A man named Ozne has contacted him about selling the rare vial of poison from the fifteenth century."

"Did Señor Pedroa say anything else?" Nancy asked.

"No. But I believe he made an appointment with Señor Ozne, who is to visit him soon."

"Thank you very much for the message," Nancy said. "I'll follow it up, and I'll let you know how we progress."

After she finished talking, Nancy thought about the person who wanted to see Señor Pedroa. Suddenly an idea came to her. She jumped up and hurried to Bess and George.

"Listen to this!" she said. "A man named Ozne has contacted Señor Pedroa about a rare fifteenth-century vial of poison!"

"Ozne?" George asked, raising her eyebrows.

"You know what that means?" Nancy said excitedly.

"No, of course not."

"It's Enzo spelled backwards!"

Bess was startled. "You think he's Enzo Scorpio?"

"I'm sure of it," Nancy replied. "I'll call Señor Pedroa immediately and suggest that when Ozne arrives, he have the police arrest him."

# 15

## *The Watermark*

Señor Pedroa was amazed by Nancy's theory. "No doubt you are right," he said. "I will do as you suggest and ask the police to be here when Señor Ozne comes with the poison. I am sure that with your description I will recognize him as well as the beautiful gold filigree covering on the vial."

He said good-by but called Nancy back in half an hour. "Everything went as planned," he reported. "Señor Ozne came to me and was apprehended by the police. The vial he was trying to sell me was not the one you described. It was a cheap one, not authentic and had no value!"

Nancy was surprised to hear this. "Are the police holding the man anyway?" she asked.

"Yes. He refuses to talk and they suspect that he is, indeed, Enzo Scorpio who is wanted by the New York authorities. They will investigate. But no one knows what he did with the genuine vial that was stolen from your friend."

When Nancy repeated the conversation to her friends, the three speculated on where the valuable vial was.

"Maybe he lost it," George suggested.

"Or he could have sold it to someone else," Bess added.

"Too bad he won't talk," Nancy said. "But I'm glad he was caught anyway."

"Right," George said. "Now all we have to do is find Dolores and catch the Hoaxters!"

"Speaking of the Hoaxters," Bess said, "I'd like to know why they bother with con games when they're making a hit in the theater."

"It could be greed," Nancy said. "According to Dad there are people who are never satisfied with their money or position. They always want to be richer or greater. Often they'll resort to illegal means to gain their ends."

Bess giggled. "And that, my dear friends, is the lesson of the morning."

The other two laughed and George asked what was next on the detectives' agenda. Nancy told her that she wanted to study their copy of the first ransom note very carefully. She spread it out on a table and the girls went over it again and again.

Nancy always came back to the same conclusion. "The message has to be '$100,000 in sack to 8 by X,'" she said.

"We assumed that 8 stands for the letter H and means Howie," George spoke up. "Could it be that H and X are street names and refer to a certain intersection in Los Angeles?"

"Possibly," Nancy said. "Let me ask Mrs. Vetter if she has a map of the city."

She returned a few minutes later with a map. It was old and torn but usable. Nancy spread it out on the table and the girls looked at the street index.

"Oh, no!" Bess frowned. "Everything from O on is missing, so we can't determine whether there are any street names starting with X."

"Yes, we can," George said. "We'll have to scrutinize every inch of the map, that's all."

Each girl concentrated on part of the map. After a while Bess said, "I'm getting cross-eyed. I really feel sorry for the printer who put this together."

"And we've come up with a blank," George added. "There's no such intersection."

"Wait a minute," Nancy spoke up. "You just gave me an idea, Bess, when you mentioned the word printer. I'm going to call Señora Mendez and ask her to look for a watermark on the original ransom note."

She hurried to the phone and was soon talking to their Mexican friend. "Please hold the paper to a strong light and see if you can make out a name or design," Nancy requested.

"All right. I'll be back in a minute."

Señora Mendez was gone so long, however, that Nancy was afraid the woman had forgotten her. Finally she came back on the line.

"It was difficult to distinguish the watermark on the paper," she said, "but I believe it's a fern leaf."

"Thank you," Nancy said. "This might be a good clue. Let's hope it leads somewhere."

Señora Mendez's voice, which had been strong up to now, wavered. "Nancy," she said, "you are such a dear, and I'm putting a great deal of faith in you."

"I'll try to live up to it," Nancy assured her.

The young sleuth said good-by, then looked through the advertising pages of the telephone book. There was a long list of stationers. She copied it and asked Bess and George to accompany her on a search for the fern marked paper.

The first shopkeeper they interviewed was very obliging. He had never heard of such a watermark but looked in his order catalog. No such design was listed.

"It may have been used some time ago and is no longer being made," he said.

The girls thanked him and left. During the rest of the afternoon they visited one stationery store after another without learning anything. It was not until they inquired at the last one on their list that they had any luck.

The gray-haired manager looked thoughtful, then said, "Yes, I recall one company that used a fern design. But I don't remember the name of it. I'm sorry. Would another type of paper suit your needs?"

"I'm sure it would," Nancy replied, not wishing to reveal the reason for their inquiry. She selected a box of pale blue paper with matching envelopes, and the girls left.

"What are you going to do now?" Bess asked.

"What I always do when I get stuck on a case," Nancy replied. "Call my dad."

The girls returned to the Vetters' and Nancy phoned Mr. Drew.

"More trouble?" he asked.

"Not really," she said. "Before I ask a favor of you, did you find out anything about the Maine hotel and Silk-O-Sheen?"

"Yes, I did," Mr. Drew replied. "The hotel is legitimate. A large stack of prospectuses disappeared, however, as well as orders for stock certificates. Apparently they were stolen."

"I'm convinced of it," Nancy said. "Barker and

139

his pals got hold of the documents and are trying to peddle them illegally!"

"Right," her father agreed. "The other story about a Silk-O-Sheen fabric is fictitious. There is no such thing."

"So it exists only in the minds of Cadwell and Barker!" Nancy exclaimed.

"That is true. As a matter of fact, you might say it was a complete fabrication."

Nancy laughed. "Dad, did you mean to make that pun?"

"What do you think?"

"I think you fabricated the fabric-ation on purpose!"

Mr. Drew chuckled. "What's the favor you wanted to ask me?"

"I'm trying to find a company that makes paper with a fern watermark. So far I haven't had any luck."

"I'll work on it," her father promised, "and start immediately."

At dinner Mrs. Vetter suggested that the girls take some time off from their case and go to a comedy movie with her and her husband.

"I think that's a great idea," Bess said. "My brain's whirling like the blades of a helicopter."

"Yours could never go that fast," George teased her cousin, and the others laughed.

As soon as the meal was finished, the group set off in Mr. Vetter's big car. Five minutes later Nancy noticed that another automobile was following close behind them. She asked their host if he would mind taking a circuitous route to the theater in case they were being trailed for some sinister reason.

"I'll be glad to," he said. "Is this going to be another detective chase?"

"I hope not," Nancy replied. "But we'll soon find out if the intentions of that other driver are good or bad."

Mr. Vetter turned left, then right a few times. For several blocks the pursuer did not leave them and Nancy was convinced that her enemies were on their trail.

Finally a break came. Mr. Vetter managed to scoot through an intersection just as the light turned red. The car behind them had to stop. By the time it was able to cross the street, Mr. Vetter had turned another corner and was out of sight.

"Oh, I'm so glad to be rid of him!" Bess exclaimed in relief.

"So am I," George added. "I couldn't have kept my mind on the movie, thinking our enemies were after us again, maybe to harm us!"

Mr. Vetter parked in the lot of the large motion picture theater and the group went inside. For two hours their minds focused on the delightful comedy that unraveled on the huge screen. When the show was over, they walked into the lobby, smiles on their faces.

"Didn't you love the detective clown who always consulted his big, long necktie when he picked up a clue?" Bess asked.

The others laughed and George said, "I think he stole the show."

Suddenly Nancy stopped short. Waiting in the long line for the next show were Cadwell and Barker!

"Look over there!" she whispered to her friends. "We must . . . ."

Just then the two con men realized that they had been spotted. Nimbly they stepped out of the line and rushed through the open front door!

# 16

## *Hijackers*

The girls pushed through the crowd in the lobby, trying to reach the two con men.

"Hey, take it easy, girlie," an annoyed man called out.

"Sorry," Nancy replied and hurried on, brushing past another man.

"What's going on?" he asked. "A fire?"

"Excuse us," said Bess, who was right behind Nancy.

George was elbowing her way through the crowd ahead of the other two. When she reached the door, a guard grabbed her by the arm.

"Look, miss, you're making a nuisance of yourself!" he scolded her.

"We just saw two con men the police are looking for," George replied. "Please let me go! We want to stop them!"

"Who are you?" the guard demanded. "Plain-clothes detectives?"

"In a way," George said, as Nancy and Bess caught up to her. By the time the girls convinced the guard that they were telling the truth and he agreed to let them go, it was too late. Barker and Cadwell were out of sight!

The girls separated and ran down the street a short distance, but it was no use. The con men had vanished. Disappointed, the young detectives met Mr. and Mrs. Vetter in the parking lot and explained why they had hurried away.

"Too bad you lost your suspects," Mr. Vetter remarked. "Perhaps you should report the incident to the police."

Nancy agreed. He drove to headquarters, where the girls gave a full account of what had happened.

"Even though the two con men got away," George added, "we know for sure that they're in Los Angeles."

"Do you think they were the same people who followed you to the movies?" the sergeant on duty asked.

"Probably," Nancy answered. "After they lost us, they might have stopped for dinner and then decided to see the show."

"We'll keep an eye out for them," the sergeant promised.

When the group arrived home, the telephone was ringing. Nancy dashed to answer it and learned Ned Nickerson was calling.

"I've been trying for the past three hours to get you," he said. "Burt, Dave, and I are leaving here tomorrow morning at nine on Continental Flight 388. Will you meet us at the airport in Los Angeles?"

"We sure will," Nancy promised. "It will be wonderful to see you."

Ten minutes before the plane was scheduled to land, the girls arrived at the airport. They found a large group of people near the Continental counter. Everyone seemed to be extremely agitated and worried. Nancy asked what the trouble was.

"Flight 388 has been hijacked!" a woman blurted out.

"Hijacked!" the three girls chorused. "Where? When?"

They were told that very little was known about the holdup at this time. The hijackers, who would not reveal their names, had not given any reason for taking over the plane.

Nancy, Bess, and George were too stunned to talk for a moment. They visualized all sorts of dreadful things happening to their friends.

Suddenly Bess spotted a familiar face among the

crowd. She whispered to the others, "I see one of the Hoaxters—the sleight of hand performer. He's over there!"

Nancy and George were startled. Why was he at the airport? Was he waiting for someone?

Bess had an idea. "Nancy, you were never on stage. Why don't you find out what you can from him?"

"Like what?" Nancy asked.

"Like whom he's expecting on this flight."

Nancy hesitated. "Remember, he recognized George *before* she went on stage. I'm sure he'd recognize me. I'll have to change my appearance a little if I want to talk to him. Bess, may I borrow your scarf?"

"Sure."

Nancy took the scarf and disappeared into a rest room. When she came out, the girl detective had hidden her hair and put on a good deal of makeup, which changed her appearance considerably.

"This is terrific for an instant disguise!" George praised her.

"Let's hope so," Nancy said with a smile.

Casually she walked over to the magician, pretending to be nervous and in need of someone to talk to.

"I'm so worried about a friend who's on board," she said. "I hope he's safe. Do you, too, have a friend or relative on the hijacked plane?"

"Yes, my wife," the man replied. "She was coming here to help me with my work."

Just then a voice sounded over the loudspeaker. "Attention, please! I have good news for people expecting passengers on Continental Flight 388. The hijackers have been overpowered and no one was hurt."

A great cheer went up from the crowd and a voice called out, "Tell us more!"

The announcer, who stood at the airline counter, said that the plane would land in El Paso, Texas, where the hijackers would be turned over to the police.

"It will then refuel and continue nonstop to Los Angeles," he concluded.

The sleight of hand man, like everyone else, looked relieved. He said to Nancy, "The plane won't be here for a while. I'm going to leave and come back later." He hurried away.

To pass the time, the girls walked around the airport, looking at shops and stopping to buy flowers for the Vetters. At last the flight was announced.

"Thank goodness!" said several of the people who had gathered to welcome passengers.

Ten minutes later Bess exclaimed, "I see them! I see the boys!"

The young sleuths rushed forward to greet their friends.

"We're so glad you're safe!" Nancy cried out. "What a frightful experience you must have had!"

Burt said, "It was hair-trigger going for a while. As far as we could learn, the hijackers wanted a free ride to South America. But we never did find out why."

Ned took Nancy's arm. "Now put us to work," he said, grinning.

She laughed. "Oh, there's plenty for you to do." Quickly the girl detective outlined their case and mentioned the sleight of hand man as one of the suspects.

"His wife was aboard your flight," she added.

"Wait a minute," Ned said. "I bet I know who she is. When the hijacking was announced, she acted like a spoiled child. She made all kinds of demands, which, of course, nobody could meet, and insisted that it was extremely important for her to get to Los Angeles and help her actor husband on stage."

"Oh, that's how you found out who she is," Nancy said.

Ned went on, "She became very agitated. No one could quiet her, not even the hijackers, who threatened her."

Dave spoke up. "See that woman with the enormous blond hairdo?"

"Hm-mm, where?" George replied.

"Down there at the last ticket counter."

George strained her neck over the milling crowd. "Oh, yes, now I see her," she said after a moment.

"Well, that's the one!"

"I'll be right back," George declared and darted after the woman. "Are you the wife of one of the Hoaxters?" she blurted out when she caught up to the stranger.

"Yes. Where is he?" the woman asked gruffly.

"He told me that he would be back later. He was here for a long time, then left."

The woman stared at George. "Are you a special friend of his?" she demanded crisply.

George stepped back. "I—"

The woman gave her no chance for a reply. "You must be, or he wouldn't have told you his plans."

"You're wrong," George said quietly.

Her calmness nettled the blond woman. She began to shriek insults at George, gesticulating wildly.

George was so stunned that for a moment she was speechless. Suddenly the woman raised her hand and slapped George hard on one cheek. Before the girl could recover her wits, the stranger hit her again. George did not know what to do. Should she fight back or run away and avoid further embarrassment?

149

# 17

## A Hoax Exposed

Adroitly George dodged the blows of the irate stranger. The athletic girl had taken lessons in judo and wondered if she should use her skills now. This proved to be unnecessary, however.

"I saw the whole thing!" a guard called out as he rushed up to stop the fight. "Do you wish to bring charges against this woman?"

"I think not," George replied.

"Well, I'll have to report the incident anyway, so if you change your mind later, you can." He turned to the woman. "Your name, please."

"Mrs. Horace Browne," the woman sputtered. "My husband is a magician. He works for a famous group called the Hoaxters!"

"Lady, I don't care whom your husband works

for. It doesn't give you the right to attack people in this airport!"

Mrs. Browne stared at him in suppressed anger. Then she gave George a scorching glance, turned on her heels and walked away.

"Are you all right, miss?" the guard asked George.

"Fine."

"Okay. Then I'll go back to my post."

Nancy, Bess, and the boys had caught up to George and were aghast when they saw her reddened face.

"What happened?" Burt asked.

Quickly George explained, adding, "If that guard hadn't arrived, I would have tried one of my judo tricks on that crazy Mrs. Horace Browne . . . that's her name. So the sleight of hand man's real name is Horace Browne. You were right, Nancy, Ronaldo Jensen is only his stage name."

"That's a good clue for us," Nancy remarked.

"I'm going to have a word with that woman one of these days!" Burt muttered.

"Why did she hit you, George?" Bess asked.

"Because she thought I was her husband's girlfriend!" George replied, making a face. The others laughed.

"What a silly idea!" Bess said in disgust.

After the group had arrived at the Vetters' and were comfortably seated in the living room with little cakes and cups of steaming chocolate, Nancy told the boys about the mystery on which the girls had been working. When Ned, Burt, and Dave heard about the swindle with the temperature-controlled clothing material, they roared with laughter.

Ned remarked, "It's a wonderful idea. Anybody who could invent something like that would become a millionaire."

Nancy looked at him. "How about you? You're majoring in science. Such an invention should be easy for you!"

"Sure," Dave added. "You wouldn't mind making a million, would you?"

"And taking us all on a great trip!" George said. "How many say *aye* to that?"

"*Aye!*" the others shouted at the top of their lungs.

Ned grinned. "Okay," he said. "If I ever make a million on clothing or anything else, I'll take you all to the moon!"

When the hilarity died down, Nancy said, "I have something else to tell you." She briefed the boys on the fern-watermarked stationery.

"If you'll excuse me for a moment, I'll call Dad to see if he has any word for me yet," she added and went to the telephone. Unfortunately, Mr. Drew had not been able to track down the manufacturer. "But I'll keep trying," he promised.

"Fern watermark?" Dave said after she had hung up. "Maybe I can help you. An uncle of mine is in the printing business. He produces bank notes, fine stationery, and all kinds of high-quality paper. Shall I call him and ask if he ever heard of the design?"

"Please do!" Nancy urged.

Dave was on the telephone for some time. When he returned, the young man was smiling. The others were sure he had learned something important.

"I have an answer for you, Nancy," he said. "The Fern Printing Company is a small outfit located in Philadelphia."

"Great!" Nancy exclaimed. "I'll see if I can get the number from Information."

After several unsuccessful attempts, she was told that the firm had no listed number. Disappointed, Nancy gave up.

"Why does a legitimate business firm have an unlisted number?" she asked herself and returned to her friends. They discussed the matter. Finally she said, "I'll call the police and tell them what we know. Perhaps they can find out Fern's private number for us."

It took the Los Angeles police department a while to supply the information, but finally Nancy was told that the firm had problems with their bills and were temporarily using the direct line of the president.

"Thank you," Nancy said, writing down the number. "I'll let you know if I learn anything important."

She hung up, then dialed the number. A woman answered. "Fern Printing Company. May I help you?"

"Yes, I'm interested in a certain type of paper—"

"I'll connect you," the receptionist interrupted. "Just a minute, please."

Nancy's heart was pounding. Was she about to make a great discovery?

A few moments passed, then a man said, "Harrison speaking. Who is this?"

Nancy evaded the question. "I understand that you manufacture fern-watermarked stationery. I haven't been able to find it in the stores here in Los Angeles. Is there someone who could show me a sample sheet of the fern pattern?"

Mr. Harrison paused briefly. "I'm afraid we don't have any in stock right now but I can give you the name of someone who buys from us."

"Oh, that would be wonderful," Nancy replied.

"It's Mr. Horace Browne who lives in Los Angeles."

Nancy's heart began to pound. What an incredible revelation!

"He should be listed in the phone book," Mr. Harrison went on. "But here's his address anyway."

Nancy wrote it down quickly. "Thank you very much," she said. "I'll send you an order as soon as I've seen Mr. Browne's paper."

"Fine. It will be available soon."

Nancy rejoined her friends. "Guess what!" she said. "I found out that Horace Browne is using the fern watermark!"

"That proves the ransom note was written by him!" George exclaimed. "Nancy, what terrific evidence!"

Ned added, "Now all we do is find out his address and confront him with the proof."

"I have the address, too," Nancy said. "All we have to do is look up his number."

George went to get the phone book. But to their dismay, the young people found that Horace Browne was not listed.

"That doesn't surprise me," Ned remarked. "If he's a crook, he'd keep under cover."

"Right," George said. "It wouldn't be wise for us to call and let him know we're coming. He'd be sure to suspect something."

Nancy agreed. "Tomorrow we'll see him personally. It's too late now. Meanwhile, I have another idea. Why don't we go to the Hoaxters' show?" She turned to Ned, her eyes twinkling. "How would you like to do a little detective work at the theater?"

# 18

## Ned's Disguise

Ned smiled at Nancy. "Do you want me to go up on the Hoaxters's stage and pull a few tricks of my own?"

"In a way, yes. When they take your wallet, there'll be a piece of paper in it torn from a small notebook. In the corner will be the Vetters' phone number."

Ned's eyebrows shot up. "What for?"

"As bait. I want to get the fingerprints of the man who rifles through wallets. Afterwards, I'll dust the paper with magnetic powder so the prints will become visible."

Ned whistled, "Smart move! How to get evidence without really trying."

"That's right. Just make sure that the paper is still in your wallet when it's returned to you after the show. It will prove that the Hoaxters are the first link in the criminal chain."

Ned pretended to be puffed up with his assignment. He stuck his fingers into the armholes of his sleeveless sweater and paraded around the room. The others laughed and wished him luck.

George said, "There's only one catch. If Mrs. Browne is on stage, she may recognize you."

Nancy suggested that when they arrived at the performance the boys go in by themselves and find seats on the left of the auditorium, while the girls would sit on the right.

Ned and his fraternity brothers agreed to the plan, and Burt added, "This way we won't be connected with Nancy Drew, the well-known girl detective!"

Nancy smiled but did not reply. She decided that she must telephone Señora Mendez and find out if there had been any further word from the kidnappers. When she heard the phone ringing in the Mendez residence, Nancy had a few seconds of hope that the child might have been returned. But as soon as her Mexican friend answered, the young sleuth knew she was wrong.

"The dear child has not come back to us," Señora Mendez told her, "and we still have no idea where she is."

"Have you or Dolores's parents received any other ransom notes?" Nancy asked.

"Yes, two. But both were fakes."

"What do you mean?" Nancy asked.

Señora Mendez said that money had been requested in both of them. It had been delivered to the specified places, but was never picked up.

"Oh, Nancy, I'm so worried that Dolores may be held for another reason besides money," the child's grandmother wailed. "I was told that certain people steal children and sell them to couples who want to adopt them."

The thought horrified Nancy, but she said calmly, "I doubt that anyone would do this with a girl as old as Dolores. She would be bound to reveal her name and where she came from and would be returned to you."

Señora Mendez said this thought made her feel better. "My private detective picked up one clue that makes it seem almost certain that Dolores is in Los Angeles," she added. "He was so sure of it that he personally called the Los Angeles police and told them his suspicions."

"What was the clue?" Nancy asked eagerly.

"One of the recent ransom notes had been made up from words cut from a newspaper just as before. My detective, who lived in Los Angeles for years, remembers that one of the papers in that city uses a special type of print in its entertainment section that he has never seen anywhere else. He's positive the words were taken from that paper."

"Have you heard from the police?" Nancy inquired.

"No. But I'm worried that the kidnappers may have found out I have a detective working on the case and that he has been in touch with the police. Perhaps that is the reason they haven't returned the child. But why are they sending me fake notes?"

"Maybe they're trying to tell you that they won't play for real as long as you have the detective involved," Nancy replied. "But I suggest that you not let him go just yet. What you told me about the newspaper clue only reinforces my suspicion that Dolores is here in Los Angeles. I'd like to hunt for her a little longer."

"All right, Nancy. But please call me tomorrow and let me know if you've had any success."

After Nancy had reported her findings to the Vetters and her friends, she said, "Tomorrow we'll call on Mr. Browne who buys the fern stationery. Mr. Vetter, where is his home located?"

"It's in an area of very expensive houses with large grounds. Many of them are fenced in. You might have a hard time trying to enter."

"I'll take a chance," Nancy replied with a determined set to her chin.

After dinner that evening the six young people set off to see the Hoaxters' show. The boys walked to the corner and took a bus, while Mr. Vetter lent his car to the girls. When they arrived at the theater, it was filling rapidly. The three detectives did not see their friends.

"We'd better not look for them too hard," George advised. "If there are any spies watching us, they may catch on to our little scheme."

The girls sat down and studied their programs. They were surprised to see that a new act had been added to the performance.

"This is the one where the sleight of hand man works with his wife," Bess whispered.

Soon the show started. The girls had seen it so many times that they were not particularly interested in it until Mr. Browne, alias Ronaldo Jensen, invited members of the audience to come on stage.

George said, "I hope Mrs. Browne doesn't recognize Ned."

He himself had had the same idea. When Ned reached the stage, the girls had a hard time to keep from laughing. He was wearing a mustache and beard!

"Ned must have rented or bought them on the way to the theater," Bess said in a low tone.

Apparently Ned's disguise worked. The woman gave no sign that she had ever seen the young man before. He was relieved of his wallet by the sleight of hand man without his noticing. Then it was held up for those in the audience to see, along with handbags, watches, and jewelry.

As in previous shows the articles were taken away, and their owners told to return after the performance. Later they filed into the back room behind the stage to claim their property.

The girls, meanwhile, had gone to the Vetters' car and were already on their way home. "I hope Ned got his wallet back with the piece of paper intact," Bess said.

"We'll soon find out," Nancy told her.

After the girls arrived at the Vetters', they paced up and down the living room impatiently, waiting for the boys. Finally they walked in.

"I have it!" Ned said jubilantly. "Nancy, bring your magnetic powder!"

Nancy had already brought the small finger-print kit she carried in her suitcase. Gingerly she removed the paper from Ned's wallet and dusted it. Everyone held his breath. Would fingerprints show up?

# 19

## The Young Prisoner

"The fingerprints are showing up!" George exclaimed.

The young people watched in fascination as the blank white paper revealed the ends of fingers on two hands.

"Are they the left and right hands of the same person?" Bess asked.

No one was sure. This was one thing the police would have to decide.

"Let's go now!" George urged.

"It's too late. We'll have to wait until morning," Nancy said.

After breakfast the following day it was decided that only Nancy and Ned would go to headquar-

ters while the rest of the group helped the Vetters with various chores.

When Nancy showed the fingerprints to the chief in his office, he was impressed. "Excellent work," he complimented her. "I'll have these traced at once. Please wait outside in the lobby. I'll let you know the result as soon as I can."

Almost an hour passed before the couple were summoned back into the chief's office. He smiled at them. "These prints belong to a wanted criminal named Sam Gambro. I'd like you to look at photographs of him and see if you can identify the man."

An enormous book lay open on a side table. The chief explained that it contained mug shots of various people who either were or had been prisoners.

"Gambro is on this page. Can you identify him?"

Nancy gazed for several seconds at the picture under which was the name Sam Gambro. He was heavyset, dark-haired, and jowly.

Finally she shook her head. "As far as I know, I have never seen this man before. So I guess he's not part of the Hoaxters's group. But he could be one of the con men who work with them."

"Possibly," the officer replied. "In order to find out, this is what we'll do. I'll send a couple of detectives to the Hoaxters who, I know, are rehearsing at the theater this morning, and have my men take their fingerprints. The detectives will pose as 'The Committee for the Protection of Entertainment in Los Angeles.'"

Nancy and Ned laughed, then went home. They told the waiting group what the chief was planning to do. All of them listened eagerly for the telephone to ring. Finally it did. Nancy answered.

"Miss Drew? This is the chief calling. The fingerprints our men brought back that belong to the sleight of hand man of the Hoaxters match those of Sam Gambro. This means he and Horace Browne are the same person."

"But Browne doesn't look anything like the man I saw in the photograph!" Nancy exclaimed.

"He must have had plastic surgery and lost a lot of weight," the chief said.

"Will Browne be apprehended?" Nancy asked.

"Yes, indeed. My men are already on their way back to the theater."

When Nancy hung up, George said she was eager to watch the sleight of hand man being arrested. "Let's go to the theater, too," she suggested.

The young detectives crowded into the Vetters' car and drove off. When they arrived at the theater, they met three policemen coming out of the building.

"Where is your prisoner?" Nancy asked them.

With a chagrined look one of the officers replied, "The Hoaxters have skipped out!"

"Again!" George exclaimed.

"Yes. Not only are the performers gone, but so are all their costumes and props. They must have become suspicious when we fingerprinted them under the pretense of being 'The Committee for the Protection of Entertainment in Los Angeles.'"

The other officer spoke up. "We've already alerted all squad cars in the area. I'm sure someone will sight them. They couldn't have gone far yet."

After the officers had driven away, Dave said, "Nancy, what's next on the sleuthing program?"

"We're going to Horace Browne's house," she replied. "Remember, I got his address from the Fern Printing Company."

"Do you think he'll be there?" George asked.

Nancy shrugged. "If he's not, perhaps we can pick up a clue to where he went."

She drove to the part of town in which Browne lived. As Mr. Vetter had told them, it was a residential area with large, attractive homes. Browne's had a high picket fence around it, and the house could barely be seen from the outside. There was an entrance gate, but it was locked. Ned pushed the bell button, but no one answered.

Bess sighed. "What'll we do now?"

"Let's split up and walk around the property," Nancy suggested. "Ned and I will go to the right. The rest of you take the left. Perhaps we can find out if someone's home."

166

Quickly the young people hurried off. Just inside the fence were high hedges, and it was impossible to look over them. After Nancy had walked around the corner and partway down one side, she said, "Ned, I want to look into the garden. Would you let me climb onto your shoulders so I can peer over the fence?"

Ned bent down. "Go ahead," he said, holding out his interlocked hands for her to step into.

Nancy climbed to his shoulders and balanced herself on the side of the fence. She managed to look over the top and beyond the bushes and had a good view of the garden. On a patio she spotted a man reclining in a lawn chair. He was sound asleep.

Excitedly Nancy leaned down to Ned and whispered, "Sam Gambro, alias Horace Browne, alias Ronaldo Jensen, is sleeping not far away. We must capture him!"

"But how?" Ned asked.

"We'll have to get over the fence. If I jump to the other side, can you make it on your own?"

"Sure. No problem. Go ahead. I'll follow."

Nancy realized that she would have to clear the bushes in order not to scratch herself badly. With determination she stepped to the top of the fence, then pushed off as far as she could. With a soft thud the girl detective landed on the lawn, unhurt.

She looked over her shoulder and saw Ned take

off from the top. He jumped gracefully and in an instant came down next to her.

"Great!" she whispered.

On tiptoes they approached Horace Browne. They were about a hundred feet away, when he suddenly awakened. Turning, he spotted the couple. The next second Browne jumped from his reclining chair and sped toward the house. He vanished through a door and they heard it slam shut and lock.

The couple looked at each other. They had been so near success!

Nancy, however, was not ready to give up. She noticed another door and hurried toward it. Fortunately this one was not locked. She dashed inside with Ned at her heels.

They found themselves at the foot of a stairway. From somewhere above, they heard faint cries for help in Spanish.

"That could be Dolores!" Nancy whispered. "Come on!"

She and Ned rushed up the stairs, but halfway to the second floor, they met Mrs. Browne coming down.

"Get out of here!" she shouted. "You have no right to be in my house. I'll call the police!"

Nancy ignored the demand. She said, "Where's Dolores?"

The woman seemed taken aback. She did not reply. The cries of the child continued. "Let me out! Let me out!"

Ned pushed Mrs. Browne firmly aside, so that Nancy could continue up the stairs. Then he followed. The couple scooted upward faster than the woman could climb. They crossed the second floor hallway and followed the cries for help to the third floor.

"Help! I want to see my mommy!" came another pleading cry.

Ned glanced back to see what Mrs. Browne was doing. She seemed undecided for a moment, then started up after the couple.

At the top of the stairway, there was a narrow hallway with a door opposite the stairs. Quickly Nancy pulled on the knob, and they looked inside.

She and Ned stood appalled at what they saw. A beautiful, dark-haired little girl of nine sat on the edge of a bed, her left ankle chained to one of its front legs!

"Dolores!" Nancy cried out and rushed to the child's side. "We're friends. We came to rescue you. We'll have you out of here in a minute!"

As she hugged the little girl, and Ned sped over to help unclamp the chain, the door was slammed shut and locked. Something heavy was pushed against it.

Ned turned back and tried to open the door. It would not budge. Now not only Dolores but he and Nancy were prisoners also!

Little Dolores became hysterical. Her few moments of joy at having been rescued were gone. She was a prisoner again!

Nancy tried to soothe her and even sang a little Spanish lullaby she knew. Ned, meanwhile, was working at the locked door. Unable to budge it, he rammed his body against the wood, hoping to splinter one of the panels. His efforts were in vain!

Finally he walked over to Nancy and they conferred on what to do. There was a tiny window high up on the wall that opened on hinges. They both knew that though one of them might crawl through it, there was no way to reach the ground safely.

"I wonder what became of Bess, George, Burt, and Dave," Nancy said. "I hope they'll find a way to rescue us!"

Dolores had become quiet now. She sat on Nancy's lap and clung to her. The young detective said, "Suppose you tell me how you got here."

"I stayed in school late to help my teacher," the little girl replied. "When I came out, all my friends had gone. A strange woman walked up to me and said, 'Are you Dolores?' When I said yes, she told me that my mother was ill and had asked her to bring me home in her car."

"So you climbed in?" Nancy asked.

"Yes, in the back seat with the woman. A man was driving. I did not know who these people were. Later I found out they were Mr. and Mrs. Browne. Mrs. Browne offered me a piece of candy."

"Did you eat it?"

Dolores nodded. "Afterwards I became very sleepy. I did not wake up until I found myself lying on the bed in this room." The little girl shivered. "And chained to the foot of it. I heard Mr. Browne say we all flew from Mexico City to Los Angeles."

"That was a dreadful experience," Nancy said. "How were you treated after you got here?"

Dolores said that Mrs. Browne and another woman had taken turns looking after her. "They brought me meals and helped me take a bath. They even washed my clothes. I kept asking them when I was going home. One day Mrs. Browne got mad at me and said, 'You're not going anywhere until your rich grandmother pays us a lot of money!'"

Nancy translated what she had learned into English for Ned, who understood some Spanish, but not as much as Nancy did.

He remarked, "That candy must have contained something to put the child to sleep."

Nancy agreed. "This way they could bring her to Los Angeles without any trouble."

As she and Ned were trying to figure out how to escape, their four friends were on the way to help them. While looking over the fence and bushes, they had seen the couple approach the sleeping man in the lawn chair and had witnessed his dash into the house.

They realized that Nancy and Ned were following him, so they, too, climbed over the fence. Just before they reached the mansion, Mr. and Mrs. Browne ran out the front door carrying suitcases.

"They're escaping!" Dave exclaimed.

When Nancy and Ned did not appear, the young people became worried about them. Were they prisoners in the house?

# 20

## *Escape!*

"Hold it!" Dave commanded as the young detectives surrounded the fleeing couple.

"Get out of our way!" Mr. Browne hissed, lashing out violently.

Fists were flying for a few moments but soon the magician and his wife were subdued and led into the house again. Bess went to phone the police. Meanwhile, in the hallway, Horace Browne managed to tear himself loose and began to fight with renewed vigor. The boys realized he had some knowledge of judo. George's skills, however, matched his. She and the boys, who were steeled by years of football practice, soon had the belligerent couple under control again.

In the rear of the hall George noticed a closet with a key in the lock and suggested they secure their prisoners inside until the police arrived. Angrily the Brownes yelled and banged on the door. After a while, however, their cries subsided and they became quiet, resigning themselves to their fate.

"I hope that magician won't use any of his tricks and get out," Bess remarked.

Nancy and Ned had heard the commotion downstairs and started to pound loudly on the door of their attic prison.

"Listen!" George said. "Someone's up there. Probably Nancy and Ned!"

She and her companions were about to hurry to the third floor when a police car drove up to the house. Three officers rushed through the open door. They were the same men who had tried to arrest the Hoaxters at the theater, only to learn they had moved out.

Quickly the young people told them about their prisoners. "One is Sam Gambro, alias Horace Browne, alias Ronaldo Jensen, the magician. The other is his wife who works with him," George explained.

"Good work!" one of the officers, named Young, said admiringly. "We caught Browne's colleagues on their way out of town, but they wouldn't tell us where he was. I'm glad you found him!"

Again there was banging from the third floor as Nancy and Ned tried to make themselves heard.

"What's going on?" Officer Young asked, alarmed. "Who else is here?"

"I believe Nancy and Ned are locked up somewhere," George said. "We saw them follow Mr. Gambro into the house before we caught him."

The four amateur detectives dashed up the stairs with Officer Young and one of his partners. They found that a large chest had been pushed in front of the attic door. Quickly they shoved it aside, then raised the bolt.

Bess opened the door and everyone stopped short in utter amazement, staring at Nancy, Ned, and the little girl.

"Meet Dolores," Nancy said with a smile of relief on her face.

As the others exchanged stories, Bess cried out, "Oh, you poor child!" She knelt and hugged the little girl, who up to now had been clinging to Nancy.

In Spanish, Nancy explained to Dolores that the newcomers were their friends.

"You mean now I can go home to my mommy?" the little girl cried out.

"Yes," Nancy replied. "The police will arrest the bad people who brought you here."

Dolores was ecstatic. "Please, may I call my mommy and daddy on the telephone?"

"Indeed you may," Nancy replied.

The group hurried downstairs and in a few minutes Dolores's parents were on the line. Their daughter talked and threw kisses into the phone, promising she would be home soon.

Then she turned to Nancy. "And now I want to speak to my grandmother." Nancy put in the call, and there was a happy, excited conversation in Spanish between Dolores and Señora Mendez.

Meanwhile, Officer Young had unlocked the closet on the first floor, let out the two prisoners, and snapped handcuffs on them.

"Before you take the Gambros away, may I ask them a few questions?" Nancy requested.

At this the couple winced and the magician said, "You know?"

"Yes," the young detective replied.

"Ask them all you want to," Officer Young said, "but let me read them their rights first."

When he finished, Nancy looked straight at the sleight of hand man. "Was it one of your con men who swindled our friend Mrs. Annabella Richards out of $3000 for a phony world trip?"

Gambro scowled. "I'm telling you nothing!"

"I think you should," his wife spoke up. "Officer, won't it be better for us if we cooperate?"

"I can't promise you anything, but I'll put in a good word for you if you make our investigation easier," Young replied.

Gambro hung his head. He realized that the game was up and shrugged. "It was Howie Barker. He pretended to be a travel agent named Henry Clark."

"And who waylaid Roscoe and stole Mrs. Richards's limousine?" Bess inquired.

"Howie and Lefty Cadwell. I told them that was a stupid thing to do. They had trouble getting rid of the car and finally put it in my garage," Gambro replied.

George asked, "When I came on stage at your show in New York, why wouldn't you let me stay?"

"After Howie tried to sell your friend space in the Maine hotel, he told me you were staying with Miss Eloise Drew. I'd read about Nancy Drew and became suspicious. Somehow Howie found out you knew Mrs. Richards. I called her housekeeper and she confirmed that you girls were detectives."

"Who rammed our taxi in New York when we left my aunt's apartment?" Nancy questioned.

"One of my co-workers," the sleight of hand man admitted. "He was supposed to keep an eye on the place and scare you enough so you'd go back home. Unfortunately, he didn't do a good job."

"You also had people watch us in Los Angeles at the Vetter home!" George accused Gambro. "Once a car followed us but we outmaneuvered it. And one of your men set a fire in the Vetters' laundry wing!"

Gambro nodded. "Too bad I had such inefficient associates," he grumbled. "Their attempts to frighten you off the case always failed!"

Bess spoke up. "Why didn't you return Dolores after the first ransom was paid?"

The prisoner scowled. "That was my wife's idea. She thought we could get more money out of Señora Mendez. Instead, we got into heaps of trouble!" He sent his wife a searing glance.

She retorted, "We wouldn't have if your man in Mexico City had collected the second ransom so we could leave Los Angeles as planned!"

"How could he? Señora Mendez had the cops on him!"

"I know there was a hidden message in the ransom note," Nancy spoke up. "'$100,000 in sack to 8 by X.' What did it mean and whom was it for?"

"It was for our Mexican contact who collected the money. He was to deliver the sack to Howie Barker on the 24th of this month."

"That was yesterday," George pointed out. "Did Barker get the ransom money?"

Gambro suddenly realized that besides going to

prison he would also lose his share of the ransom. He became sulky.

"Why should I tell you any more?" he growled. "I've confessed too much already."

Further questioning netted no more information, so two of the police officers took their prisoners to headquarters. Officer Young remained behind.

Nancy asked him, "Would it be possible for us to search the house? Perhaps the $100,000 is hidden here."

Young smiled. "You're in luck. When we found out that the Hoaxters had left the theater, we obtained a warrant to look for clues in any suspicious places. We haven't used it yet."

"Terrific!" Nancy said. "Let's split up and search every inch of this house."

The young people and the police officer examined each room and scrutinized all the furniture. At one point George cried out, "Come here, everybody! I've found the stolen vial of poison!"

The others stared at it in amazement. Bess exclaimed, "This is definitely the one Enzo Scorpio stole from Mrs. Richards!"

"You're right," Nancy agreed. "I recognize the filigree."

George added, "Enzo must have sold it to Sam Gambro, then tried to palm off a cheap imitation on Señor Pedroa! Well, I'm glad Enzo is in prison, and Mrs. Richards will be happy to get her vial back."

The search went on with renewed interest. Ned found a letter indicating that the two con men, Howie Barker, alias Ralph Rafferty, alias Henry Clark, and Lefty Cadwell were staying at a hotel in San Francisco. The letter also revealed that the name of the ransom collector in Mexico City was Alfredo Scorpio. He was the father of Enzo and a cousin of Gambro.

"Now I get it!" George cried out. "Enzo got in touch with Gambro and sold him the poison!"

The officer agreed. "I'll relay this information to headquarters at once!"

While he was busy, the young people completed their search. Nothing more turned up, and the hiding place of the ransom money remained a mystery.

Nancy suggested that they leave and take Dolores to the Vetters. On their way out, she had an idea.

"Let's take a look at Mrs. Richards's limousine which is supposedly in Gambro's garage," she suggested.

Officer Young locked the front door and everyone went to the garage. Mrs. Richards's car was there, with the keys under the floor mat. The group searched it quickly and Nancy asked Ned to open the trunk. There was nothing inside except the spare tire. Ned lifted it out. A sack lay underneath!

Excitedly Nancy pulled the drawstring. Bundles of money fell out!

"The ransom!" she exclaimed. "Dolores, we've found your grandmother's money!"

The little girl clapped her hands and Nancy scooped Dolores up in her arms. Everyone was overjoyed to have recovered the $100,000, which was quickly counted. All of it was there.

Officer Young asked, "Will you give me a ride to headquarters? I'm sure the chief will be surprised when I walk in with all this money!"

When Nancy and her friends arrived at the Vetters' house, the couple, who spoke Spanish, immediately made little Dolores feel welcome. Everyone played games with her and much to the child's delight a meal was served consisting partly of Mexican dishes.

While they were eating, Dave asked, "Nancy, have you thought of a name for this mystery?"

The girl detective was silent for a few moments, then replied, "Yes. I'll call it *The Triple Hoax*. The first one that the Hoaxters pulled was to defraud Mrs. Richards. The second one was to kidnap Dolores."

"And the third?" Ned asked, puzzled.

Nancy grinned. "You perpetrated the third hoax when you went up on stage at the show and permitted your wallet to be taken. From the paper inside we obtained the fingerprints of the sleight of hand man which wound up the case."

Secretly Nancy wondered if she would ever have another case to work on. But a new one, called *The Flying Saucer Mystery*, was soon to come her way.

That evening, Nancy received a surprise telephone call from the chairman of the convention of U.S. detectives.

"We understand that you and your friends are amateur sleuths," he said. "We would like you to attend our banquet tomorrow evening."

The young people were delighted with the invitation. "We have a little girl with us," Nancy said. "Will it be all right to bring her along?"

"Indeed it will," the chairman replied. "We'll expect you all at seven o'clock."

The next day Nancy, George, and Bess bought Dolores a complete new party outfit. At six thirty the group took a limousine taxi to the banquet hall.

The headwaiter checked the visitors' names at the door, then led them through a maze of tables. Finally he pointed to where Nancy and her friends were to sit. They stopped short in amazement.

A large group was gathered at the table, including Mr. Drew, Hannah Gruen, Aunt Eloise, Mrs. Richards, the Vetters, Señora Mendez, and a couple who were introduced as Dolores's parents. "Surprise!" they cried as the little girl rushed to her family.

Nancy's face wore a broad grin. "How wonderful!" she said. "Who arranged this get-together?"

Her father said the chairman had learned from the police that Nancy and her friends had done a fine job solving the mystery, and the detectives wanted to show their admiration.

During dinner, everyone chatted gaily. Mr. Drew said that the two checks sent to the suspicious mail order houses had bounced as expected.

"Those companies were phony and their officers have been arrested. They were part of the widespread Hoaxter outfit."

When the meal was over, the chairman stood up and gave a speech that made Nancy blush. He described the young sleuths' work in uncovering the illegal schemes of the Hoaxters and the con men, all of whom had been apprehended. Then he mentioned the missing vial of poison that had been recovered and the arrest of Enzo Scorpio and his father, Alfredo.

Finally he asked Dolores to stand up. He told the audience how she had been kidnapped and that

Nancy Drew, with the help of Bess, George, and their friends from Emerson College, had found the child and restored Dolores to her family.

"Nancy, we detectives want you to have something to show not only our admiration but our thanks for such a wonderful job," he declared and reached down alongside his chair. He pulled up a framed award stating exactly what the girl detective had done.

"How marvelous! Thank you!" she exclaimed.

As he presented it to her, there was loud applause, a standing ovation, and wild cheering from Nancy's many admirers.

You are invited to join

THE OFFICIAL NANCY DREW™ FAN CLUB!

Be the first in your neighborhood to find out about Nancy's newest adventures in the *Nancy Drew™ Mystery Reporter,* and to receive your official membership card. Just send your name, age, address, and zip code to:

**The Official Nancy Drew™ Fan Club
Wanderer Books
1230 Avenue of the Americas
New York, NY 10020**